THE BURGLAR

Harbin was thirty-four and he had been a burglar for the last eighteen years. It wasn't much of a life, but it was a living. Then Harbin met Della, a woman so mesmerizing that he just couldn't say no.

THE BURGLAR

by
David Goodis

MAGNA PRINT BOOKS
Long Preston, North Yorkshire,
England.

British Library Cataloguing in Publication Data.

Goodis, David, *1917—1967*
The burglar.
I. Title
813.52 (F)

ISBN 1-85057-815-X
ISBN 1-85057-816-8 pbk

First Published in Great Britain by Simon & Schuster Ltd., 1988.

Published in Large Print 1990 by arrangement with Simon & Schuster London and the copyright holder.

Printed and bound in Great Britain by
Redwood Press Limited, Melksham, Wiltshire.

CHAPTER I

At three in the morning it was dead around here and the windows of the mansion were black, the mansion dark purple and solemn against the moonlit velvet green of gently sloping lawn. The dark purple was a target and the missile was Nathaniel Harbin who sat behind the wheel of a car parked on a wide clean street going north from the mansion. He had an unlit cigarette in his mouth and in his lap there was a sheet of paper containing a diagram of burglary. The plan gave the route aiming at the mansion, moving inside and across the wide library to the wall-safe where there were emeralds.

In the parked car Harbin sat with his three companions. Two of them were men and the third was a blonde skinny girl in her early twenties. They sat there and looked at the mansion. They had nothing to express and very little to think about, because the mansion had been thoroughly cased, the plan had been worked and re-worked with every move scheduled on a split-second basis, the thing discussed and debated and rehearsed until it was a fine, precise plan that looked to be foolproof. Harbin told himself it was foolproof, allowed that to simmer for a while, then bit hard on the cigarette and told himself nothing was foolproof. The haul was going to be risky and as a matter of fact it might prove to be more risky than any they had ever attempted. It was certainly the biggest haul they had ever attempted and it was these big hauls that offered the most danger. Harbin's thinking went that far and no further. He was inclined to pull the brakes on thinking when his mind began looking at risk.

Harbin was thirty-four and for the past eighteen years he had been a burglar. He had never been caught and despite the constant jeopardy he had never been forced into a really tight corner. The way he operated was quiet and slow, very slow, always unarmed, always artistic without knowing or interested in knowing that it was artistic, always accurate with it and always extremely unhappy with it.

The lack of happiness showed in his eyes. He had grey eyes that were almost never bright, subdued eyes that made him look as though he were quietly suffering. He was a rather good-looking man of medium height and medium weight and he had hair the colour of ripe wheat, parted far on one side and brushed flat across his head. His mode of attire was neat and quiet and he had a soft quiet voice, subdued like the eyes. He very seldom raised his voice, even when he laughed, and he rarely laughed. He rarely smiled.

In that respect he was on the order of Baylock, who sat next to him on the front seat of the car. Baylock was a short, very thin man in his middle forties, getting bald, getting old fast with pessimism and worry, getting sick with liver trouble and a tendency to skip meals and sleep. Baylock had bad eyes that blinked a lot and small, bony hands constantly rubbing together with worry and the memory of several years ago when there was prison. Baylock had been in prison for what he considered a very long time and on certain occasions he would talk about prison and say what an awful thing it was and claim that he would rather be dead and buried than be in prison. Most of the time Baylock was a bore and sometimes he could really get on one's nerves and at certain times he was truly intolerable.

Harbin could remember specific occasions when he had been fed up with Baylock, finally weary of Baylock's continual whining and nagging, the sound of complaining and pessimism that was like a dripping faucet, going into the nerves and going in again and again until the only thing to do was walk away from Baylock and keep on walking away from him until he got tired of hearing himself talk. Baylock always took a long time to get tired of that, and yet Baylock was completely dependable during a haul, valuable after a haul because of his ability to appraise loot, and valuable mainly because all his motives and all his moves were always displayed out in the open.

Harbin recognized and appreciated that rare trait in Baylock, and so did the others, the two in the back seat, the girl and Dohmer. Although Dohmer at times showed active hostility towards Baylock, it was a temporary hostility that always bubbled and climbed and blew up and died. Dohmer was a tall, heavy Dutchman, touching forty, with a wide, thick nose and a thick neck and a thick brain. The brain never tried to accomplish what it knew it couldn't accomplish and for that reason Dohmer was just as valuable to Harbin as Baylock was. Dohmer was quite clumsy on his feet and he was never allowed to work the inside of houses, but from the outside he functioned well in the capacity of lookout and during emergencies he was more or less automatic, reacting like a network of gears and wires.

Harbin took the cigarette from his mouth, looked at it and put it back in again. He turned his head to look at Baylock, then went on turning his head to look at Dohmer and the girl. The girl, Gladden, looked back at Harbin and as their eyes met and held there was a moment of strain and difficult waiting, as though this was as far as it could go, this thing of just looking at each other and knowing it couldn't go any further than just this. Glow from a streetlamp far back came through the rear window, came floating in to settle on Gladden's yellow hair and part of her face. The glow showed the skinny lines of her face, the yellow of her eyes, the thin line of her throat. She sat there and looked at Harbin and he saw her skinniness, this tangible proof of her lack of weight, and in his mind he told himself she weighed tons and tons and it all hung as from a rope around his neck. He looked at this burden that was Gladden, tried to smile at her but couldn't smile because he saw her in that moment as a burden and nothing more than a burden, then drew himself up and away from that moment and saw her only as Gladden.

Only as Gladden she was quiet and kind and it was pleasant to have her around. When it came to the hauls she was completely mechanical and went through her manoeuvres as though she was knitting. On all the hauls she did all the casing and she did it in a relaxed, somewhat detached manner that made it look almost easy although it was really very difficult, sometimes more difficult than the haul itself. On this haul, aiming at something around a hundred thousand dollars worth of emeralds in a wall safe, Gladden had worked for six weeks to get in good with certain servants who worked in the house, to get into the house on the pretext of visiting with the servants when the family was away for a weekend, to line up the information and take it back to Harbin and Baylock and Dohmer. She did all that with each move carried out according to plan, getting her directions from Harbin, asking no questions and going through with the directions exactly as specified, coming back with all the facts she was told to obtain, and just standing there quietly when Baylock began to whine and nag and complain. Baylock said she should have come back with more, there were undoubtedly more burglar alarms than the ones she had listed. Baylock said it was an unsatisfactory job of casing. But then Baylock was always getting his digs in at Gladden.

There was nothing personal in the digs. Baylock was really fond of Gladden and when they weren't working on a haul he was amiable toward her and he showed her a kindness now and then. But the hauls were the big things in Baylock's life and he saw Gladden as a drag, her femininity a negative force working against the success of the hauls, and even if the hauls were successful, Gladden was a woman and sooner or later a woman causes grief and Baylock was constantly taking Harbin aside and drilling away at this issue. Gladden was Baylock's major complaint though he never made the complaint bluntly in her presence. He would wait until she wasn't around, and then he would start on it, this favourite complaint of his, telling Harbin that they didn't need Gladden, they ought to give her some money and send her away, and she would be better off and most certainly they would be better off.

Harbin always did his best to change the subject, because this subject was something he not only didn't want to talk about, it was something he didn't want to think about. He knew he couldn't convey to Baylock the reasons why they had to retain Gladden. The reasons were deep and there were times when he tried to study them and could not figure them out himself, could only see these reasons as vague elements floating in sinister depth, his contact and relationship with Gladden a really weird state of affairs, something about it that was unnatural, and it was like a puzzle that threw itself in front of one's eyes and stayed there, wouldn't go away, persisted there and grew there. He had gone through countless nights when there was no sleep, only the black ceiling of a room above his eyes, the thought of Gladden a hammer that dangled from the ceiling and clanged against his brain. It was as though he could see the hammer, its metal shining against the darkness of the room, the force of it swinging towards him, coming hard, coming into him. And it was as though he was tied there hand and foot and there was no getting away. The thing was planted. It was set. There was no getting away from Gladden.

Looking at her now, seeing her face there in the rear of the car, he made another attempt to smile at her. He couldn't smile at her. But she was smiling at him. There was sweetness in her smile, soft and gentle and yet it was a blade going through him and he had to turn his head away. He bit into the cigarette and wished he could light it, but they had their own rules about lighting matches during a haul. He shifted the cigarette across his mouth and glanced at his wristwatch.

Then he turned to Baylock and said, 'I guess we're ready.'

'Check your tools?'

'I'll check them now,' Harbin said, and from his coat pocket he took a small metal sliver that could have been a fountain pen, and pressed the edge of it and tested the light it stabbed to the floorboards. From another pocket he took a flannel case tied with a shoelace, undid the shoelace, took out the little tools one by one and held them close to one eye, the other eye closed, studying the fine tips and edges of the tools, touching the smooth metal with a forefinger, closing both eyes to concentrate on the feel of the cold, accurate metal against his flesh. It was wise to always check each tool just before the beginning of a haul. Harbin had learned long ago that metal is an unpredictable element and sometimes it chooses embarrassing moments to give way.

The tools seemed to be all right and he had them back in the case and put the case in his pocket. He glanced again at his wristwatch and said, 'All right, get your eyes wide open.'

'You going now?' Dohmer said.

Harbin nodded and opened the door and stepped out of the car. He crossed the wide smooth black street, came onto the curving pavement bordering the flowers of the lawn of the mansion. Coming onto the lawn he moved toward the window that had been selected.

Again the flannel case came out of his pocket and from the case he took an instrument designed to cut glass. The glass-cutter did its work quietly as Harbin turned the little lever putting the little blade in motion. Finally the glass-cutter sliced a small rectangle permitting Harbin to get his fingers inside to open the window lock. He had the window going up slowly and quietly. He told himself that just about now Gladden ought to arrive. There was a sound near him, and he turned and looked at Gladden. She smiled at him, then a quick gesture with her right hand, something like brushing a fly away from her nose, signified that Dohmer and Baylock were now in their specified placements. Dohmer was at the rear of the house, watching the rear upstairs windows, to see if and when a light would go on. Baylock was on the lawn up toward the front, where he could watch the front and side windows, and where he could get a good view of the street and their parked car. It was very important to keep an eye on their parked car. The police along Philadelphia's Main Line knew most of the cars in this section of mansions, and would be inclined to check any cars that looked like strangers.

Harbin lifted a finger toward the window, and Gladden climbed in. Light from Harbin's small flashlight streaked under her arm as he followed her in. She took the flashlight from him and he followed her across the room toward the wall-safe. No attempt had been made to camouflage the safe and the flashlight displayed it as a square of hammered brass, centred with an ornamental combination dial. Harbin nodded slowly and Gladden went back to the window to stand there where she could watch for flashlight signals from Dohmer and Baylock.

At the safe, Harbin took another look at his wristwatch. He gazed at the safe, ignoring the combination dial and concentrating on the edge of the brass square. He glanced again at his wristwatch and gave himself five minutes at the outside. He began chewing on the unlit cigarette as he removed the important tool from the flannel case.

The important tool was a tiny circular saw revolved by a pumping process, in the order of a hypodermic syringe. The teeth of the saw bit through oak that panelled the brass square. Harbin had his face close to the oak, but every now and then he took it away to see if there was any green light on the wall near him. The green light would be from Gladden's flashlight, in case she needed to use it. The chances were he would see the signal anyway, if it came, but he had to be sure, because here her flashlight threw a wire of green glow, and if it wasn't aimed just right, he would miss it. But if the green light did come, it would mean that Gladden had received an alarm from either Dohmer or Baylock or both of them. It would mean that Dohmer would come running to the window, to climb in and intercept anyone coming down from upstairs, to use the special brand of Dohmer technique to silently yet firmly quiet the intercepting party. Or possibly it could mean interception coming from the outside and Dohmer and Baylock would be forced into a decoy set-up. It could mean a great many things and Harbin had all the potentials carefully listed in his brain.

The saw finished one side of the square. The rhythm of the saw made a sound something like that of a man groaning deep in his throat. It was a night sound and it could be an insect out there in the springtime air. Or it could be the distant sound of an automobile. It was a sound that Harbin had tested many times at the Spot, and Gladden had used the saw downstairs while Harbin, his head against the pillow, strained his hearing, and threw aside all rationalization, and finally decided the sound was passable. At the Spot they were always going through this sort of testing, and they practised constantly.

They all hated the practising, especially Harbin, but it was Harbin who quickly stifled all arguments against the practising.

Three sides of the square were sawed and he was on the final side when grass-on-fire came into his eyes. He turned and saw the bright green flame from Gladden's flashlight. It went on and off, on again, stayed on, then three bursts from it and he knew there was disturbance on the outside and Baylock had given the signal and it was police and they were at the parked car. He opened his mouth just a little, the chewed cigarette fell out from between his teeth, bounced off his elbow and hit the floor. He leaned over and picked it up, his eyes seeking Gladden at the window, waiting for more from her flashlight. He saw her standing there at the window, giving him her profile in what was almost silhouette. For such a skinny girl, he told himself, she had reasonable height, somewhere around five feet three. She really ought to put on some weight, he told himself. She had an appetite like a wren. The police, he imagined, were now walking around the parked car. He imagined their bandit chaser was parked beside the car and now they were walking around it and looking at it and not saying anything. Now they were inside it. They would see the interior of the automobile. They were tremendous, these police, because the next thing they would do was to look at each other. Then they would look around the night air. They would just stand there. The police, he told himself, were marvellous when it came to just standing there. Sometimes they elaborated on it a little and pushed their caps back and forth on their heads. Nobody could push a cap back and forth on his head like a policeman. He went on looking at Gladden and waiting for more from her flashlight. Her flashlight stayed dark. Harbin looked at his wristwatch. The next time he looked at his wristwatch it was eight minutes later and he knew he must do something about the policemen, because the lack of further news from Gladden meant the police were still out there.

He moved across the room, came toward Gladden.

He stood beside her profiled face and said close to her ear. 'I'll go out.'

Her only movement was breathing. She kept her eyes on a garden wall where lights from the other flashlights would show. She said, 'Tell them what?'

'Car broke down,' he said. 'I went to look for a mechanic.'

For some moments she had no reply. He

waited to hear something. It was a real emergency, yet whatever she said wouldn't mean anything to him in a practical sense, because he was going out anyway. But he liked to know his ideas were solid, and he wanted her to say this was solid. He handed her the tools and his flashlight. He waited.

She said, 'You always underestimate the cops.'

It wasn't the first time she had said that. It didn't annoy him. Perhaps it was true. Perhaps it was actually a serious weakness in his campaigning, and some night it would truly backfire. But it remained a perhaps and he was never affected strongly by the possible or even probable. The only merchandise he ever bought was the definite.

He said, 'Watch your diet,' just to say something before he climbed out. Then he was through the window and out on the lawn, working close to the house, getting toward the rear. Shrubbery came up in front of his face and he circled it and saw Dohmer crouching near the stone steps leading to the kitchen door. He made a little sound through the corners of his mouth. Dohmer turned and looked at him. He gave Dohmer a small smile, then moved on, passing Dohmer, working his way around to the other side of the house, cutting across the lawn and seeing Baylock pressed hard against a wall of the garage on the far side of the lawn. He came up behind the garage, edged his way in toward Baylock, making just enough noise so Baylock could hear him coming. Baylock moved a little, stared at him. He nodded and Baylock returned the nod. He faced around, retraced his steps to bring himself on the other side of the garage. Then there was more shrubbery. He went through it. Another line of shrubbery brought him down near the end of the driveway, toward a curving street lowering its way around the north side of the mansion. He came out and onto the street, took off his coat, opened his shirt collar, put a cigarette in his mouth and struck a match.

Puffing at the cigarette, he walked up the street, holding his coat over one arm, then made the turn at the summit of the climbing street. It brought him in view of the parked black car and the parked red car and the two policemen.

They stood there and waited for him. He sighed and shook his head slowly as he walked up to them. One of them was large and past forty and the other was a young handsome man with pale blue eyes, like aquamarine.

The large cop said, 'This your car?'

'I wish it wasn't.' Harbin looked at the car

and shook his head.

'What you doing around here?' the young cop said.

Harbin frowned at the car. 'Know where there's an all night mechanic?'

The large cop rubbed his chin. 'You kidding?'

The young cop looked at the black car. It was a 1946 Chevrolet sedan. 'What's wrong with it?'

Harbin shrugged.

'Let's see your cards,' the large cop said.

Harbin handed his wallet to the large cop and watched the young cop walking around the Chevrolet and examining it as though it was something new in the zoo. Harbin leaned against a fender and went on smoking his cigarette as he watched the large cop looking through the cards and checking them with the licence plates. He saw the young cop opening the front door on the other side and sliding in behind the wheel.

The large cop handed back the wallet and Harbin said, 'I must have walked a couple of miles. Nothing. Not even a gas station.'

'You realize what time it is?'

Harbin looked at his wristwatch. 'Jesus Christ.'

From inside the car, the young handsome

cop said, 'Where's your keys?'

'What do you mean?' Harbin said.

'I mean where's your keys? I want to try it.'

Harbin opened the front door next to the steering wheel, reached in toward the ignition lock and found only the lock. He frowned up at the long nose of the young cop. He withdrew himself from the car, threw a hand toward his rear trousers pocket, then went through the act of searching for the keys, telling himself he didn't like the eyes of the young cop.

The young cop came out of the car and folded thick arms and watched him as he searched for the keys.

'God damn it,' Harbin said. Now he was going through his coat pockets.

The young cop said, 'How come you lose keys?'

'They're not lost,' Harbin said. 'They got to be around somewhere.'

'Been drinking?' The young cop moved in a little.

'Not a drop,' Harbin said.

'All right then,' the young cop said, 'where's the keys for your car?'

Instead of answering Harbin leaned his head inside the car, under the steering wheel and began to search on the floor for the keys. He heard the young cop saying, 'You look at his cards?'

'They're in order,' the large cop said.

A hand touched Harbin's shoulder, and he heard the young cop saying, 'Hey.'

He came out from underneath the steering wheel. He faced the young cop. He said, 'Some nights a man just shouldn't go out.'

Again the young cop had his arms folded. His aquamarine eyes were lenses. 'What do you do?'

'Installment business,' Harbin said.

'Door to door?'

Harbin nodded.

The young cop glanced at the large cop and then he turned his handsome face toward Harbin and said, 'How do you make out?'

'I break even,' Harbin pushed a weak grin onto his lips. 'You know how it is. It's a struggle.'

'What ain't?' the large cop said.

Harbin rubbed the back of his head. 'I must have had the keys in my hand when I got out of the car. Must have dropped them while I was walking.' He waited for the policemen to say something and when they didn't he said, 'I might as well crawl in the back and go to sleep.'

'No,' the young cop said, 'you can't do that.'

'Can you run me into town?'

The young cop pointed to the red bandit chaser. 'Does that look like a taxi?'

Harbin put his hands in trousers pockets and gazed dismally at the street. 'Might as well go to sleep in the car.'

There was a long wait. Harbin kept his eyes away from their faces. He had a feeling the young cop was watching him closely. He knew it was now at the point where it would go one way or another, and all he could do was wait.

Finally, the large cop said, 'Go on, get in your car. The night's half shot anyway.'

Harbin crossed in front of the aquamarine eyes of the young cop. He opened the rear door of the car, climbed in, curled up on the upholstery and closed his eyes. Around a minute later he heard the engine of the red car starting up. He heard the red car going away.

The long hand on his wristwatch travelled for seven minutes before he raised his head to peer through the car window. Turning the handle that brought the window down, he listened for engine noise, but the night air was empty of sound. He inhaled the quiet, enjoying it. Then, climbing out of the Chevrolet, he put another cigarette in his mouth and moved toward the mansion.

Gladden was at the window as he climbed in.

He gave her a grin while she handed him the tools. He turned on his flashlight, aimed it at the wall safe, followed the path of white light across the room to the square of hammered brass, and beyond the brass, the emeralds.

CHAPTER II

They were looking at the haul. The four of them were on the second floor of a small dingy house in the Kensington section of Philadelphia. The house was in Dohmer's name and it was very small, part of a narrow street of row houses hemmed in by factories. The house was their dwelling place, their headquarters, and they called it the Spot. Dust and dirty air from the mills was always coming in even when the windows were closed. Gladden had a habit of throwing a cleaning-rag at the windows and saying it was no use trying to fight this dust. After awhile she would sigh and pick up the rag and go on with the cleaning.

The table in Baylock's room on the second floor was in the centre of the room and they stood around and watched Baylock as he examined the emeralds. Baylock's fingers were pincers of thin metal as he picked up the gems one by one and held them against the glass fitted into his left eye. Dohmer had beer going down his throat from a quart bottle, and Gladden's hands were clasped behind her back, her shoulders resting slightly against Harbin's chest, the smoke from his cigarette spraying through the yellow hair of Gladden and floating toward the centre of the table where the stones flamed green.

After a while Baylock took the glass from his eye and picked up a piece of paper on which he had been making an itemized list with the estimated value of each jewel. 'Come in around a hundred and ten thousand. Cut the stones down, melt the platinum, shape it up again and it ought to bring around forty.'

'Forty thousand,' Dohmer said.

Baylock frowned. 'Less the expenses.'

'What expenses?' Dohmer said.

'Overhead,' Baylock said, biting at the corner of his mouth.

Harbin looked at the emeralds. He told himself it was a nice haul and he ought to feel good about it. He wondered why he didn't feel good about it.

Baylock said, 'We better move this rapid.' He got up from the table, walked up and down, came back to the table. 'I figure we go tomorrow. Pack up in the morning and start out. Take it down to Mexico.'

Harbin was shaking his head.

'Why not?' Baylock asked.

Harbin didn't answer. He had his wallet out and he was tearing the operator's licence and registration card in little pieces. He turned to Dohmer. 'Get new cards printed and take care of the Chevvie. Get it done fast. Get new upholstery, now, new paint job, melt the licence plates. Everything.'

Dohmer nodded, and then he said, 'What colour you want it?'

Gladden said, 'I like orange.'

Harbin looked at her. He was waiting for Baylock to commence an argument about Mexico. He knew Baylock would have something to say about Mexico.

'Make it a dull orange,' Gladden said. 'I don't like bright colours. They're cheap. They're common. When I buy dresses, I buy them in soft colours. With good taste. With class. Make the car a smoky orange or a grey orange or a burnt orange.'

Dohmer took the beer bottle from his mouth. 'I don't know what you're talking about.'

'I wish,' Gladden said, 'sometime I could get to talk with women. If once a month I could talk lady talk with ladies I'd be happy.'

Baylock rubbed fingers across his balding head. He frowned down at the emeralds. 'I figure we go tomorrow and head for Mexico City.'

'I said no,' Harbin let it come cool.

As though Harbin had not spoken, Baylock said, 'Tomorrow's the best time to go. Soon as we get the car changed over. Go down to Mexico City and get the stuff to a fence. Get it done rapid.'

'Not tomorrow,' Harbin said. 'Not next week. Not next month.'

Baylock looked up. 'How long you want to wait?'

'Between six months and a year.'

'That's too long,' Baylock said. 'Too many things can happen.' And then for some unknown reason he looked directly at Gladden and his eyes became almost closed. 'Like stupid moves. Like painting the car bright orange.'

'I didn't say bright orange,' Gladden said. 'I told you I didn't like bright orange.'

'Like getting up in society,' Baylock went on. 'Like getting in with the servants on the Main Line.'

'You leave me alone,' Gladden said. She turned to Harbin. 'Tell him to leave me alone.'

'Like getting high ideas,' Baylock went on. 'With good taste. With class. First thing we know she'll be in circulation.'

'Now you shut up, Joe,' Gladden cried. 'You got no right to talk like that. I got in with the servants 'cause that's the only way I could case the place.' Again she turned to Harbin. 'Why does he pick on me all the time?'

'God, first thing we know,' Baylock said, 'she'll be up in the world with Main Line society. We'll have rich people coming up here to play bridge and have tea and look at our emeralds.'

Harbin turned to Gladden, 'Go out in the hall.'

'No,' Gladden said.

'Go on,' Harbin said, 'go out and wait in the hall.'

'I'll stay right here.' Gladden was quivering.

Baylock frowned at Gladden and said, 'Why don't you do like he tells you?'

Gladden turned fully upon Baylock. 'You shut your God damn lousy face.'

Harbin felt something twisting around in his insides, something getting started in there. He knew what it was. It had happened before. He didn't want it to happen again. He tried to work it down and stifle it, but it kept moving around in there and now it began to climb.

Baylock said, 'I claim we start tomorrow. I claim—'

‘Drop it,’ Harbin’s voice sliced the room. ‘Drop it, drop it—’

Gladden said, ‘Hey, Nat—’

‘You, too,’ Harbin was up from the chair, he had the chair in his hand, up in the air, high up, then heaving the chair against the wall, moving towards the dresser and picking up a half-empty bottle of beer, bashing it to the floor. He took his fist and slammed it into the air. His breathing sounded like broken machinery. He was pleading with himself to stop it, but he couldn’t stop it. They stood there and looked at him as they had looked at him many times when it had happened before. They didn’t move. They stood there and waited for the thing to die down.

‘Get out,’ he shouted. ‘All of you, get out of here.’ He threw himself on Baylock’s cot, his fingernails cutting through the sheet, then the sheet underneath, his fingers tearing at both sheets as he arched his back to destroy the fabric in his hands. ‘Get out,’ he screamed, ‘get out and leave me alone.’

They worked their way out of the room. He was on his knees, on the cot, tearing the sheets, ripping them until they were scraggly ribbons. He fell on his side, rolled off the cot, hit the table so that it went off balance and the gems splattered on the floor. He was on the floor among the emeralds, his flesh touching them without feeling them. He closed his eyes and heard voices in the hall. Dohmer's voice was loud, getting louder against the loudness of Baylock's voice. Gladden yelled something he couldn't make out, but he knew what was happening. He wanted to remain there on the floor and let it grow and let it finally happen. He picked himself up from the floor, and as he heard the shriek from Gladden, he staggered across the room toward the door.

He was in the hall, throwing himself between Dohmer and Baylock, getting in low to put his arms around Dohmer's knees, his shoulder against Dohmer's thigh, his feet bracing hard, then the push and the heave as his arms went even lower so that he took Dohmer with him to the floor.

Dohmer's eyes didn't see him. Dohmer was gazing past him, up at Baylock. There was a good deal of grief on Baylock's face. Baylock's left eye was swollen and purple and the eyebrow was cut.

Rising slowly, Harbin said, 'All right, it's over.'

'It isn't over.' Baylock was weeping without tears.

'If you feel that way,' Harbin said, 'don't stand there thinking about it. Here's Dohmer right in front of you. If you want to hit him, go ahead and hit him.'

Baylock had no reply. Dohmer had risen and now stood rubbing his brow as though he had a severe headache. A few times he opened his mouth, wanting to say something, but he was unable to choose words.

Gladden lit a cigarette. She gave Harbin a scolding look. 'This is all your fault.'

'I know it is,' Harbin said. Without looking at Baylock, he murmured, 'Maybe if certain people would stop needling me, it wouldn't happen.'

'I don't needle you,' Baylock wept. 'All I do is say what I think.'

'It isn't thinking,' Harbin said. 'It's crying the blues. You're always crying the blues.' He gestured toward the bathroom. 'Fix him up,' he said to Gladden, and she took Baylock into the bathroom. Harbin turned and moved into the bedroom and began putting things back in order.

In the doorway, Dohmer rubbed palms across his knuckles. 'I don't know what got into me.'

Harbin set the table on its legs. He put the chair back in place. He gathered the scattered gems and when they were all collected and in their cloth on the table, he turned to Dohmer and said, 'You make me sick.'

'Baylock makes you sick.'

'Baylock makes me sore. You make me sick.'

'I didn't mean to do it,' Dohmer said. 'I swear I didn't really mean to hit him.'

'That's why you make me sick. As long as you do what you mean to do, you're a utility. But when you lose your head you're worse than nothing.'

'You're the one went out of control.'

'When I go out of control,' Harbin said, 'I punch air, I don't punch a face.' He pointed to the torn sheets. 'I damage that. I don't damage the people I work with. Look at the size of your fists. You could have killed him.'

Dohmer moved into the room and sat on the edge of the cot. He went on rubbing his knuckles. 'Why do these things have to start?'

'Nerves.'

'We've got to get rid of that.'

'We can't,' Harbin said. 'Nerves are little wires inside. They stay there. When they're pulled too tight, they snap.'

'That ain't good.'

'Nothing you can do about it,' Harbin said, 'except try to steer it when it happens. That's what I try to do. I try to steer it. Instead of aiming that hand at Baylock, you should have aimed it at the wall.'

'I'm too big,' Dohmer stood there very dismally. He looked with pleading at Harbin. 'You've got to believe me, Nat, I got nothing against Baylock. I like Baylock. He's been very good to me. He's done me more favours than I can remember. So look what I go and do. I walk in and slam my hand into his eye. This hand here,' and he displayed his right hand, holding it out as though offering it to be cut off.

Harbin saw Dohmer's hand go down, the immense shoulders slumped, the big head descending into cupped hands. Something midway between a moan and a sob came from Dohmer's throat. It was evident that Dohmer wished to be alone with his remorse, and Harbin walked out of the room and closed the door.

He entered the bathroom to see Baylock with head tilted far back under the light above the washbowl. Gladden pressed gently with a styptic pencil, then she held the white pencil under cold running water, then applied it again. Baylock made a thin sound of pain.

'It's awful,' Baylock said. 'It's like fire.'

'Let me see.' Harbin stepped in close to examine the eye. 'Not too deep. You won't need stitches, anyway.'

Baylock gazed morosely at the floor. 'Why did he have to hit me?'

'He feels worse about it than you do.'

'Does he have this eye?'

'He wishes he did,' Harbin said. 'He feels lousy about it.'

'That helps the eye a lot,' Baylock whined.

Harbin lit a cigarette, taking his time. Then, after a few puffs, he looked at Gladden. 'Go downstairs and fix us something to eat. Later on I'll take you out for a drink.'

'Should I dress up?' Gladden asked. 'I'd love to dress up.'

Harbin smiled at her.

She said, 'I get a real kick when I'm all dressed up. What I like best is that number with the silver sequins. You like that one, Nat? That yellow dress with the sequins?'

'It's very pretty.'

'I'm dying to wear it tonight,' Gladden said. 'I got a real itch to take that dress out and put it on and wear it. Then I'll be out with you and I'll be wearing that dress.'

'Nice,' Harbin nodded. 'Real nice.'

'It's always real nice when I'm all dressed up in a dress I'm crazy about, and I'm sure crazy about that sequin thing. I'll put it on and I'll be wearing it when we go out, and I'll have it on and I'll feel fine. I feel real good just thinking about it.'

She was walking out. They heard her as she reached the head of the stairs, saying aloud to herself, 'Just thinking about it.' They heard her going down the stairs.

'That there,' Baylock said, 'is something I can't make out.' He was forgetting his bad eye and looking directly and thoughtfully and probing at Harbin, and saying, 'It ain't me that gets on your nerves. It's the girl. The girl always gets on your nerves. The girl is a dumbbell and you know she's a dumbbell. I think it's time you did something about it.'

'All right,' Harbin waved wearily. 'Cut that.'

'She's dumb,' Baylock said. 'She's plain dumb.'

'Why don't you drop it?'

'Look at it, Nat. Take a look at it. You know I got nothing personal against Gladden. She's straight and she means well but that ain't the point. The point is, she's dumb and you know it just like I know it. The difference is, I come out with it and you hold it back inside. You choke yourself up with it and that's why you broke loose tonight and went haywire. I can't take it any deeper than that, but I know it goes way deeper.'

'Can't we just leave it like this?'

'Sure we can,' Baylock said. 'Another thing

we can do is close up shop.'

'You're walking a wire, Joe. I don't like what you're saying.'

'I'm saying what I know to be a fact. You got things you want to do and I want to be with you when you do them. Dohmer too. But with the girl it's another play. Everything she does, she does because you tell her to. Using her own brains, she couldn't move an inch, anyway not in the direction we take. There's trouble there, and sooner or later it blows right up in your face. Don't tell me you don't see it coming.'

Harbin opened his mouth wide, shut it tight, then opened it again. 'You trying to give me the creeps?'

'You already got them.'

Then Harbin's voice was down to almost a whisper, 'You be careful.'

Baylock's manner went into an abrupt change. 'What the hell's wrong,' he whined. 'Can't I even disagree? If you make a point and I don't see it your way, I have the right to come out with it, don't I?'

'It's always something,' Harbin said. 'No matter what I say, with you it's no. Everything is no.'

'I can't agree when I don't agree.'

'All right, Joe.'

'I can't help it,' Baylock said. 'That's the way it is.'

'All right.'

'I don't want to keep harping away, but I keep worrying about that girl. She has a real wrong effect on you and it's got to the point where I always know when it's up to your neck.' He moved in close to Harbin, 'Let her go.' He moved in closer, his voice low. 'Why don't you let her go?'

Harbin turned away. He took in some stale air and swallowed it with an effort and a certain pain. 'We're an organization. One thing I won't allow is a split in the organization.'

'It wouldn't be a split. If you told her to go, she'd go.'

'Where would she go?' Harbin's voice was loud again. 'What would she run into?'

'She'd be all right,' Baylock said. 'And I can tell you one thing. She'd be a lot better off than she is now.'

Harbin turned away again. He closed his eyes tightly for a moment, wished he was sound asleep and away from everything.

Baylock was close again. 'You know the way it is with you? As though you've been in some courtroom and got yourself a life sentence to take care of her.'

'God damn it,' Harbin said, 'leave me alone.'

He walked out of the bathroom. He came into the room where Dohmer was still sitting on the cot with his big head covered by big hands. Baylock came in a few moments later. The two of them stood there, watching Dohmer.

Dohmer slowly lifted his head. He looked at them, he sighed heavily and began shaking his head. 'I'm so sorry, I'm so sorry, Joe.'

'It's all right,' Baylock let a hand rest for a moment on Dohmer's shoulder. And then his eyes moved and came to a stop on Harbin, and he added, 'I wish everything was all right.'

Harbin bit hard at his lip. He felt his head jerking to one side. He couldn't look at either of them.

CHAPTER III

In an after-hour club that gave out membership cards for five dollars a year, the light from pale green bulbs tossed a watery glow on Gladden's hair. The glow was on the top of her head, floating there. Her head was bent toward the tall glass with the rum and ice in it, and Harbin watched her as she sipped the drink, smiled at her as she lifted her head and looked at him. They sat at a very small table away from the centre of activity, an absurdly small dance floor faced on the other side by three Negro musicians who constantly played with all their might. The place was on the second floor of a Kensington Avenue restaurant, and it kept its lights low, its customers happy, its blue-uniformed visitors paid off promptly each week. It was a pretty good place.

'They give us a nice drink,' Gladden said. 'Like the music?'

'Too jumpy.'

'What kind of music do you like?'

'Guy Lombardo.'

'I used to play the violin,' Harbin said.

'No.'

'But I did,' Harbin said. 'I took lessons for five years. There was a conservatory in our neighbourhood. They'd take in twenty kids at a time. We'd all be in a little room with the old guy up front, and he'd scream at the top of his lungs as if we were all a mile away and he was trying to make himself heard. He was a maniac, the old guy. I wonder if he's still there.'

'Tell me,' Gladden said. 'Tell me about the neighbourhood.'

'I've told you a thousand times.'

'Tell me again.'

He picked up the short glass and swallowed some whiskey. He beckoned to a coloured girl who was walking in and out through the tables with a big tray above her head. 'Why?'

'I get dreamy.'

The coloured girl was at the table and Harbin ordered a few jiggers of whiskey for himself and another rum collins for Gladden. He leaned back in his chair, his head to one side a little as he studied the pale green glow on the top of Gladden's head. 'Always,' he said, 'after we do a job you get dreamy like this. The haul doesn't seem to interest you.'

Gladden said nothing. She smiled at something far away.

'The haul?' he said, 'becomes a secondary thing with you. What comes first?'

'The dreamy feeling,' Gladden slumped languidly. 'Like going back. Like resting back on a soft pillow that you can't see. Way back there.'

'Where?'

'Where we were when we were young.'

'We're young now,' he said.

'Are we?' Her tall glass was lifted, her chin magnified through the rum and soda and glass. 'We're half in the grave.'

'You're bored,' Harbin said.

'I've been bored since I was born.'

'You looking for kicks?'

'Who needs kicks?' She gestured toward the dancers crowding the tiny floor. 'They're all crazy.' She shrugged again. 'Who am I to talk? I'm crazy, too. So are you.'

Harbin saw the pale green glow coming down a little and making a wide pale green ribbon across her forehead. Now her yellow hair was a zig-zag of yellow and black, her eyes under the ribbon a distinct and bright yellow, her face dark but getting lighter as the ribbon lowered, and Harbin saw the whiteness of her teeth as she smiled again. He returned the smile, not knowing why. And then, not knowing why, he said. 'You want to dance?'

She pointed to the slow chaos on the dance floor. 'Is that dancing?'

He looked at it and it wasn't dancing. He listened to the music and it gave him nothing. He threw a drink into his stomach and there was no tingle. He looked at Gladden and she was watching him and he knew she was studying him and he said, 'Let's leave.'

She didn't move. 'You tired?'

'No.'

'Then where will we go?'

'I don't know, but let's get out of here.' He started to rise.

'Wait,' she said. 'Sit down, Nat.'

He sat. He had no idea of what she intended to say. He waited for it with a nervousness that bothered him greatly because there really was no reason for it. Finally he said, 'You're terrific when it comes to times like this.'

'Nat.' She leaned her elbows on the table. 'Tell me. Why do you go out with me? Why do you take me places?'

'I like company.'

'Why not Dohmer? Why not Baylock?'

'You're better to look at than they are.'

'You go for scenery?'

'You're not bad.'

'Don't be sweet to me, Nat. Don't give me compliments.'

'It isn't a compliment. It's a statement.' He didn't care for the direction this talk was taking. He shifted a bit in his chair. 'I'll tell you what I would like. I'd like to see you enjoy yourself once in a while. Times I look at you and you look like hell.' He leaned toward her, his arms flat on the table. 'What I want you to do is go away for a while.'

'Go where?'

'Anywhere. Baltimore. Pittsburgh. Atlantic City.'

'Atlantic City,' she mused. 'That would be all right.'

'Sure it would. You really need a rest. You'll

get out on the boardwalk and sit there in the sun and breathe some salt air. Do you a world of good. Get to bed early and put some decent food in your stomach. Put some colour in your face.'

Her face was coming closer to him. 'You want to see some colour in my face?'

'You'll take in some shows,' he said, 'and go for rolling chair rides on the boardwalk. You can lie down on the beach and get that sun—'

'Nat,' she said.

'And you can go for boat rides. They have boat rides out on the ocean and at night you can walk on the boardwalk and they have some smart shops where you can buy those dignified dresses you're always talking about.'

'Nat,' she said. 'Nat, listen—'

'They have these smart shops on the boardwalk and you'll have yourself a fine time.'

'Nat,' she said. 'Go with me.'

'No.'

'Please go with me.'

'Stop being stupid, will you?'

She waited awhile, and then she said, 'All right, Nat, I'll stop being stupid. I'll do what you want me to do. What you expect of me. I'll turn it off, just like that,' and she imitated the turning off of a faucet. 'I'm good at that. I've practised and practised and now I know how.' Once more she turned the imaginary faucet.

'Tomorrow,' he said, 'you'll grab a train.'

'Fine.'

'Atlantic City.'

'Marvellous.'

He put a cigarette in his mouth and began to chew on it. He took it out and bent it and broke it and let it fall in the tray. 'Look, Gladden,' he started, and didn't know how to continue. The line of his thinking refused to stay on one path, and split up like a wire coming apart and branched off wildly in countless directions. He saw the coloured girl passing the table and he touched her arm and said he wanted the cheque.

CHAPTER IV

There was no phone at the Spot, and the next afternoon, at three, while they waited at the station for the Atlantic City train, they decided that she should make calls to a certain drugstore booth at stipulated intervals. Then the train arrived, and he stood back as she entered the train. Suddenly she put down her bags and faced him and said his name.

He grinned. 'Don't fill up on salt water taffy.'

'We haven't said goodbye.'

'When you go to China we'll say goodbye.'

She gave him a look he couldn't classify. Then other passengers were crowding him in, and there was no more time. He turned, walked down along the platform. Descending the steps leading to the waiting room, he heard the train going away. It occurred to him that this was the first time he had seen Gladden going away, and for some odd reason it was disturbing. He told himself Atlantic City was only sixty miles away. It was the place where Philadelphians went to get the sun and the salt air. It wasn't China. It was practically right next door, and he would be in constant touch with Gladden. There was no reason for him to be disturbed.

He stood outside the terminal and wondered where he should go. It was always a problem, where to go and what to do. Sometimes he came close to envying the people whose lives were based on compulsory directives, who lived by definite need and command, so that every morning they had to get up at six or seven, and be at a specific place by eight-thirty or nine, and stay there and do specific things until five or six. They never wondered what to do next. They knew what they had to do. He had nothing to do and no place to go. He had plenty of money to spend, around seven thousand dollars remaining from his share of the two previous hauls, but he couldn't think of a way to start spending it. There was nothing special that he wanted. He tried to think of something that he wanted, but a wall came up in his mind and blocked off everything tangible.

So he went back to the Spot because there was no other place to go. The Spot was reassurance. The Spot was security. In its own strange way, the Spot was home.

Entering, he heard Baylock's voice from the kitchen. He walked into the kitchen. Baylock and Dohmer were at the table, playing their original variation of two-handed poker. Dohmer showed a hole card, an ace that matched another and gave him the hand. Dohmer collected a dollar and seventy cents, and then they put aside the cards and looked at Harbin.

Baylock said, 'She go?'

'Took the three-forty.' Harbin looked out the window.

They were quiet for a few moments. Dohmer let out a big yawn. Then he pointed to the window and said, 'Look at that sun. Look at that sun out there.'

'Let's go romp in the park,' Baylock said. He scowled at the cards. He picked them up and shuffled them, riffled them, stacked them and shuffled them again and put them down.

Harbin stood at the kitchen window and looked at the sunlit sky above the alley and the grey dwellings. He was thinking of Atlantic City, picturing the boardwalk and the beach and the beach-front hotels.

Dohmer said, 'I think I'll have something to eat.'

'You ate an hour ago,' Baylock said.

'So now I'll eat again.'

Dohmer and Baylock went on arguing, and Harbin stood at the window, gazing out at nothing. He thought about Gladden and her father, and about himself. He thought of when he was a little boy in a little town in Iowa, an only child, his father a merchant of dry goods, his mother a timid, soft-voiced, sweet-souled woman who tried hard to like everybody. When her husband died she took over the business and did what she could with it and finally lost it. There came a day when she had to borrow money, a day when she had to borrow more, a day when the son heard her weeping in a dark room, and a day when a chest cold became pneumonia and she didn't have the strength to fight it. She lasted only a few days. He was in high school at the time. He didn't know what to do. The world was an avalanche, taking him down, and he found himself on a road going away from the little town. He was sixteen years old and during that year he wandered and groped and resented and feared. It was the year when a good many people were hungry, and it was known generally to be very bad times. He almost starved to death that year. He would have starved to death if it hadn't been for a man named Gerald Gladden.

The thing took place in Nebraska and Gerald Gladden was driving south from Omaha, accompanied by his six-year-old daughter. Gerald was approaching middle age and he was a paroled convict who now felt sure he had learned enough to continue the science of burglary without getting caught. It was late in the day when he saw the boy with lifted thumb begging for a ride. His car whizzed past the boy and then in the rear-view mirror he saw the boy sagging to the ground. He put the car in reverse and picked up the boy.

That was the way it started. The way it exploded was raw and unexpected. Harbin had just passed his nineteenth birthday and he and Gerald went on a second-storey job in the suburbs of Detroit. A shrewdly concealed burglar alarm went off and some ten minutes later police bullets hit Gerald in the spine and then a slug smashed through his brain and that was the end of him. Harbin had better luck. Harbin worked his way back to the rooming house where the little girl was asleep and for the first time in his three-year association with Gerald he took a good look at Gerald's daughter. This was a tiny, sad little girl whose mother had died while giving birth to her. This was Gerald Gladden's daughter. It occurred to Harbin he had an obligation. When he edged his way out of Detroit a few weeks later, he took the little girl with him. A month after, in Cleveland, he had a birth certificate and some other papers drawn up by an individual who specialized in this sort of thing, and the little girl was officially designated as his kid sister. He couldn't think of a good first name for her, so he decided on Gladden. The last name was unimportant. It was the name he was using then, and unimportant because he was changing his name every time he entered a new town. He enrolled Gladden in an inexpensive private school and went out and found a job selling kitchen utensils on a door-to-door basis. For five years he stayed away from burglary. He sold the kitchenware, door-to-door, and averaged about thirty-five dollars a week, and it was just about enough for Gladden and himself. Then one day he met Baylock, and Baylock introduced him to Dohmer, and a few nights later they were out on a job.

The amazing thing was the war. They had ways and means to get out of all sorts of situations, but they couldn't evade the war. It was fast and blunt, the way the Army snapped them up. Only Baylock could sidestep the Army, because Baylock had a record and also a bad set of kidneys. Baylock offered to take care of Gladden while Harbin was away. Baylock had a sister in Kansas City, and Gladden went to live with the sister and Harbin went away to war.

Then five years passed and the war was ended and Harbin came back. Dohmer was already back and doing jobs with Baylock. That was something Harbin expected. What he hadn't expected was to see Gladden being used on the jobs. They were using Gladden for jobs that required inside work. Gladden was now nineteen, and she was still tiny and still sad and she seemed unhappy with what she was doing, and Harbin had no idea of what to say. He had a feeling she was waiting for him to say something, and after awhile he knew what it was she wanted. She wanted him to say this was no good, they must get out of it now, he would go back to selling kitchenware door-to-door, and she would get herself a job washing dishes or something. But he couldn't say it.

They made rather large hauls but they couldn't accumulate much money. They began having trouble with the fences. Baylock couldn't get along with the fences. Then Baylock got into the habit of involving other individuals in the projects and this developed until there were a great many people who for various reasons had to be paid off. Finally Baylock managed to complicate things to the point where they were in actual jeopardy, not from the law, but from these other people, and it was Harbin who took over then and smoothed things out. That made Harbin the leader. Baylock began screaming his head off, and he made so much noise that Harbin finally told him he could have the leadership back again. But Dohmer and Gladden refused to accept this, and Baylock eventually admitted that Harbin was best fitted to run the projects. But now Baylock was beginning to complain about Gladden. And another thing, Baylock said, Harbin's operations were too slow.

Harbin was really very slow. It took him weeks to plan a job and then more weeks before the job was activated. Then it took months before the fence was contacted. Then it took more months until the deal with the fence was consummated. But this was the way Gerald had taught him to operate, and most of what he knew he had learned from Gerald. With Gerald it was a science and a business and Gerald had learned it from a wizard who had finally gone to Central America with close to a million dollars in ice-cold money and had died there an old man. Gerald had always dreamed of accomplishing the same feat, had always claimed it could be done and it would be done provided one could learn the science of taking one's time and knowing all the grooves and potentials before making a move. With Gerald that was the big thing, the patience, the waiting, and yet even Gerald had succumbed to the poison of impulsiveness. That night in Detroit the death of Gerald could have been avoided if Gerald had only waited another fifteen or twenty minutes, if he had taken the time to look for additional wires that meant auxiliary burglar alarms. Gerald had thirty-odd dollars in his pocket when he died, but as he hit the ground with his bullet-slashed skull he was pointing his body toward Central America, his hands reached out, clutching for the million dollars in ice-cold money.

CHAPTER V

All the rest of the day Harbin stayed at the Spot. It suddenly became evident that with Gladden absent there was no housekeeper, and Harbin put himself to work straightening things out, dusting around in a more or less spiritless way. Dohmer sprawled in a dingy sofa and supervised Harbin's work between gulps of beer. Baylock stood in a doorway and suggested Harbin should put on an apron. Harbin suggested it might be a damn good idea if they shook their legs and helped out. For a couple of hours the three of them swept and dusted. Gradually the momentum of the work became an attraction in itself, they began to scour and scrub, and the Spot was considerably the cleaner except for the places where Dohmer worked. Dohmer succeeded in upsetting a bucket of soapy water. Harbin told him to clean up the mess and he opened a window and said the sun would dry it out. He then flopped on the sofa and claimed he was completely exhausted.

Toward seven o'clock, Harbin left for the

phone booth to receive the scheduled call from Gladden. The drugstore was on Allegheny Avenue, going away north from Kensington. They had chosen the second booth from the left in a row of four. He entered the booth at two minutes to seven, sat there smoking a cigarette and deliberately calling a wrong number. At seven o'clock the phone rang in the booth.

Gladden's voice from Atlantic City was low and he told her to talk louder. She said her hotel room was very nice, looking out on the ocean, and she was going to buy herself a good dinner and then take in a movie and get to bed early.

Then she said, 'What are you doing?'

'Nothing in particular. I'm sort of tired.' He wasn't the least bit tired. He couldn't understand why he had said it.

She said, 'Tired from what?'

'We cleaned up the Spot today. Now it's almost fit to live in.'

She said, 'Tell Dohmer not to start with cooking. Once he begins in that kitchen we'll have a regiment of cockroaches. You know what I'm seeing tonight? A Betty Grable picture.'

'She's good.'

'It's with Dick Haynes.'

'Yeah?'

'It's all in colour. With a lot of music.'

'Well,' he said, 'enjoy the picture.'

'Nat?'

He waited.

She said, 'Nat, I want to ask you something. Look, Nat. I want to ask you this. I want to know if it's all right if I go out.'

'What do you mean, if you go out? Sure you can go out. Aren't you going out tonight?'

'Tonight I'm going out alone. And tomorrow night I guess I'll be going out alone. But maybe one of these nights I'll go out with somebody.'

'So?'

'So is it all right?'

'Fine,' he said. 'If you're asked out, you'll go out. What's wrong with that?'

'I just wanted to make sure.'

'Don't be sappy. You don't have to ask me these things. Just use your own judgment. Now look,' he added quickly, 'you won't have enough change to pay this phone bill. Hang up and call me same time tomorrow night.'

He put the receiver on the hook. Walking from the drugstore he picked up an *Evening Bulletin* and his eyes were on the headline as he dropped a nickel in the slotted cigar box. The headline said it was a hundred-thousand-dollar burglary and there was a picture of the mansion. He tucked the paper under his arm. A few minutes later, in a small restaurant, he began reading the story while telling a waitress to bring him a steak and some french fries and a cup of coffee. The story said it was one of the slickest jobs ever pulled on the Main Line and there were absolutely no clues. They didn't mention the two policemen and the parked car near the mansion, and this of course was understandable because mentioning it would make the police look like idiots.

He finished the paper and worked on his steak, and watched the other customers. His eyes worked their way toward two middle-aged pudding eaters, and across the room to a lonely young man, then toward the woman who sat at a nearby table, then toward three girls who were sitting together, then quickly back to the woman, because the woman was looking at him.

He couldn't be sure whether she was smiling. Her lips were relaxed and so were her eyes. He sensed there was something international in the way she sat there, looking at him. It wasn't bold, it wasn't what he would call cheap. But it was a direct look, coming right at him. For a moment he figured perhaps the woman was deep in her own thought and had no idea of what she was looking at. He turned his head away, tried that for a few seconds, then brought his eyes back to hers. She was still looking at him. He noticed now she was something out of the ordinary.

It began with the colour of her hair. Her hair was a pale tan, not blonde, and he would swear it wasn't dyed. It was glistening tan hair. She wore it tight and flat on her head, parted far on one side, then brushed back to her neck where he saw the edge of a little brown ribbon. The eyes were the same colour as the hair, the special tan, and the skin was perhaps a shade lighter. He told himself either she was an expert with a sunlamp or her beautician was a wizard. The nose was thin yet not stingy, taking up just about the right amount of room on her face, a graceful oval of a face unlike any face he had ever seen. He could see her body was slender, and there was something sleek about it even though her attire made no effort at sleekness. The longer he looked at her, the more certain he was that he ought to stop looking at her.

He knew if he kept on looking at her he would start getting fascinated, and it was almost a religion with him, his refusal to allow himself to be fascinated by any of them. He pulled his eyes away from her and just to do something he began toying with the strap of his wristwatch.

Across the room, someone put a nickel in the music machine and a weak, whispery baritone begged the world to show pity because a girl in an organdie dress had gone away and would never come back. Harbin finished the steak and lit a cigarette while he creamed his coffee. He found himself becoming quite restless. He decided to go downtown and shoot some pool at one of the large, respectable places. Then he changed his mind, sensing there might be something better to do. Maybe he ought to visit the public library. He liked it in the library, the big one on the Parkway, where it was an endless flow of quiet and calm and he could sit there reading the thick volumes dealing with precious stones. It was a very interesting subject. Many times he had imitated the people he saw there in the library with their notebooks, doing research. He had brought a small notebook to the library and made notes from the books on precious stones. Tonight, he told himself, would be a good night to go to the library. He started to get up from the table, keeping his eyes on the door but knowing he would turn his head just for one more look. He turned his head. He looked at her and her eyes were on him.

She was only a few feet away, but her voice

seemed to be coming from a distant area. 'Enjoy your meal?'

He nodded very slowly.

'I don't think so. You didn't seem to be enjoying it.'

Without moving from where he stood, he said, 'You do this all the time? Visit restaurants to see if people enjoy their food?'

The woman said, 'Maybe I've been rude.'

'You're not rude,' Harbin said. 'You're just interested.' He moved toward her. 'What makes you interested?'

'You're a type.'

'Special?'

'Special for me.'

'That's too bad.' Harbin smiled. He smiled as kindly as he could.

He had a feeling she had been married at least twice, and he was ready to bet she had a man now and at least three more on the string. He asked himself, what did he need this for? He had always avoided this and why was he allowing it to grab at him now? The answer came, rapid and keen. Never before had he seen anything that even approached this.

'If you're looking for company,' he said, 'you can come along with me.'

'Where?'

'All right,' he said. 'Forget it.'

He turned his back on her, moved to the cashier's stand. He paid his check, left the restaurant and stood on the corner waiting for a cab. The night air had a thick softness and the smell of stale smoke from factories that had been busy in the day, and the smell of cheap whiskey and dead cigarettes and Philadephia springtime. Then something else came into it and he breathed it in, and he knew the colour of this perfume was tan.

She stood behind him. 'Usually I don't gamble like this.'

He faced her. 'Where would you like to go?'

'Maybe someplace for a drink.'

'I don't feel like a drink.'

'Tell me,' she said. 'Are you hard to get along with?'

'No.'

'You think we can get along?'

'No.' A cab rolled through the middle of the street, and he beckoned to it. Entering the cab, Harbin told himself he had handled it the way it should have been handled, and any other way would have been a mistake, and as it was, he had made enough of a mistake in even beginning to talk with her. He started to close the door, but she was already climbing into the cab, and he found himself sliding across the seat to make room for her.

The driver leaned back. 'Where we going?'

'The Free Library,' Harbin said. 'On the Parkway.' He studied her and for a few moments she gazed frontward, then slowly turned her head and looked at him. She smiled and her mouth opened just a little. He could see her teeth.

She said, 'My name is Della.'

'Nathaniel.'

'Nat.' she said. 'That's an all right name for you. It's soft but it has a snap to it. A soft snap. It's a patent leather name.' She pulled in some smoke and let it out. 'What do you do for a living?'

'Do you really want to know, or are you just trying to make talk?'

'I really want to know. When I'm interested in a man, I want to know all about him.'

He nodded a bit dubiously, 'That's either a good policy or a very bad one. You let yourself in for a flock of disappointments. Suppose I told you I was a shoe salesman and I made forty a week?'

'You'd be lying.'

'Certainly,' he said. 'I'm much too smart to sell shoes for a living. I have that snap quality, that soft snap. Tell me all about it. Tell me the story of my life so far and what I should do with the rest of it.' He frowned at her with nothing in the frown but honest curiosity. 'What is it you want? What are you out for?'

'Basically?' She was no longer smiling. She held the cigarette close to her mouth but she had forgotten it. Her eyes were slightly wide, as though she was surprised at the reply she was about to give. 'Basically,' she said, 'I'm out to find myself a lover.'

The impact of it was like the initial touch of an oncoming steamroller. He told himself to get back on balance. The presence of women in his life had never represented much of a problem, although the potential was always there, and he could always see the potential. He had always found it not at all difficult to sidestep and manoeuvre himself away from annoying involvement. The thing was purely a matter of timing. To know just when to walk out. And he knew as sure as he was sitting here, this was the time to walk out. Right now. To tell the driver to stop the cab. To open the door and slide out, and walk away, and keep walking.

She held him there. He didn't know how she was doing it, but she held him there as though she had him tied hand and foot. She had him trapped there in the cab, and he looked at her with hate.

'Why?' she said. 'Why the look?'

He couldn't answer.

She said, 'You frightened?' Without moving, she seemed to lean toward him. 'Do I frighten you, Nat?'

'You antagonize me.'

'Listen, Nat—'

'Shut up,' he said. 'Let me think about this.'

She nodded slowly, exaggerating the nod. He saw her profile, the quiet line of her brow and nose and chin, the semi-delicate line of her jaw, the cigarette an inch or two away from her lips, and the smoke of the cigarette. Then he took his eyes and pulled them away from Della, and then without looking at Della, he was seeing her. The ride to the library took up a little more than twenty minutes, and they weren't saying a word to each other, yet it was as though they talked to each other constantly through the ride. The cab pulled up in front of the library and neither of them moved. The driver said they were at the library, and neither of them moved. The driver shrugged and let the motor idle and sat there, waiting.

After a while, the driver said, 'Well, what's it going to be?'

'The way it's got to be,' she said. As she floated her body toward Harbin, she gave the driver an address.

CHAPTER VI

It was up in the north of the city, in a section known as Germantown. To get there, the cab had to follow the Schuylkill River, following the night sheen of the river up along the smooth river-drive and curving away and following Wissahickon Creek and then past the rows of little houses of working people who lived on the outskirts of Germantown. The cab went deep into Germantown and finally pulled up in front of a small house in the middle of a badly lighted block.

The inside of the house was a combination of creamy green and dark grey, the green predominating, the furniture green, the wallpaper the same green, the rugs dark grey. It was an old house that had been done over. Above the fireplace, within a wide tan frame, there was a line drawing of Della's face, and it was done in tan tempera on very pale tan boardpaper. The artist's name was on the Spanish side.

Harbin said, 'You have a lot of money, don't you?'

'A fair amount.'

He turned away from the line drawing. 'Where'd you get it?'

'My husband died a year ago. Left me an income. Fifteen thousand a year.'

She had seated herself in a deep sofa that looked like it was fashioned from pistachio ice cream and would melt away any minute. He started toward the sofa, then moved to one side, kept moving in that direction, stopped when he reached a wall. 'How do you spend your time?'

'Miserably,' she said. 'I sleep too much. I'm sick and tired of sleeping all the time. One of these days I'll open a shop or something. Come over here.'

'Later.'

'Now.'

'Later.' He remained there facing the wall. 'Got many friends?'

'None. No real friends. Just a few people I know. I go out with them and the evening starts to drag and it gets to a point where I feel like lighting firecrackers. I can't stand people who aren't exciting.'

'You find me exciting?'

'Come over here and we'll find out.'

He gave her a little smile and then he looked at the rug. 'Aside from that,' he said, 'what do you figure we can offer each other?'

'Each other.'

'Entirely?'

'Everything,' she said. 'I wouldn't have it any other way. This you've got to know about me. The first time I was married I was fifteen. The boy was a couple years older and we lived on neighbouring farms in South Dakota. We were married a few months and then he got run over by a tractor. I went out to look for another man. It wasn't the idea of marriage, exactly, it was just that I needed a man. So I found me a man. And then another. And another. One after another. And each had something to offer, but it wasn't what I wanted. I've always known what I wanted. Six years ago when I was twenty-two, I got married for the second time. That was in Dallas and I was selling cigarettes in a night club. The man was married and he was down there for their first real vacation in ten years. He was forty and worth a fortune. Copper mines in Colorado. He started running around with me and finally his wife went back to Colorado and got a divorce. The man married me. After four years of it he began getting on my nerves. He started with the jealousy. That's all right, the jealousy, when it's carried out with finesse. You know the soft snap. It's attractive that way. But with him it was all red hot temper. He threatened to tear my head off. One night he hit me in the face. With his fist. That was just a little more than a year ago. I told him to pack up and go to the other side of the world. He went out and a few days later he threw himself off a fishing boat. I started looking for another man. All my life I've been looking for a certain man. You think I should keep on looking?'

He didn't say anything.

'I want it now. I want an answer.'

'It takes time.'

'Don't bore me,' she said. 'Don't stand there thinking it over.' A certain rigidity came into her voice. She behaved as though they were in the midst of a crisis. 'I've waited for tonight. I've waited a long time. I sat there tonight and watched you at that table. I watched you eating your dinner. And I knew. Not the trace of a doubt.'

He glanced at his wristwatch. 'We've known each other exactly two hours and sixteen minutes.'

She was up and away from the sofa and coming toward him. 'You letting that wristwatch make your decisions? I've never been guided by time. I won't let myself be guided by it. Jesus Christ in Heaven, I know, I know, I'm standing here and telling you I know. And you know, too. And if you deny that, if you doubt it, if you can't make up your mind right now, I swear I'll throw you out of here—'

Closing in on her, he smothered her mouth.

The liquid of her lips poured into his veins. There was a bursting in his brain as everything went out of his brain and Della came in, filling his brain so that his brain was crammed with Della. For a single vicious moment he tried to break away from her and come back to himself, and in that moment they were helping him, Dohmer and Baylock. They were helping him as he tried to pull away. But Gladden wasn't helping. Gladden was nowhere around. Gladden ought to be here, helping. Gladden was letting him down. If Gladden hadn't gone away, this wouldn't be happening. It was all Gladden's fault. He took it that far and he couldn't take it any further, because from there on it was all Della. It was very distant from the earth and there was nothing but Della.

A little past six in the morning he stood under a shower and let the water run as cold as it cared to. He heard her voice beyond the bathroom door, asking him what he wanted for breakfast. He told her to go back to sleep, he would get something outside. She said he would eat breakfast here. When he came downstairs, the orange juice was already fixed and she was busy in the kitchen with eggs and bacon.

They sipped orange juice. She said, 'Soon we'll do this in the country.'

'You like the country?'

'Far out,' she said. 'I already have a place. Midway between here and Harrisburg. It's a farm, but we won't farm. We'll just live there. It's a marvellous place. My car's being fixed but maybe it'll be ready by noon. We'll drive out today and I'll show it to you.'

'I can't.'

'Why not?'

'I have a couple of people to see.'

'You mean you have to work?'

'In a way.'

'How long will you be away?'

'I don't know. Talk to me. Tell me more about this place in the country.'

'It's about thirty miles the other side of Lancaster. The famous rolling hills of Pennsylvania. This is a very high hill. We're not at the top, but on the side of the hill where it has a gradual slant, then levels off for a while before it goes down again. What you see from here is all the other hills going out, the greenest hills you ever saw in your life. Then away, far away, but somehow so close that it seems right next door, we have mountains. Lavender mountains.

You see the river but before that you see the brook. It runs coming up toward you in a lot of soft easy jumps, curving up the pond that's where you can reach in and get your hand wet if you lean out the bedroom window. It's deep enough, this pond, so in the morning if you feel in the mood, you can roll yourself out the window and go into the water.'

'What do we do there?'

'We just stay there. Up there together in that place on that hill. Not a soul anywhere near. We'll be together there.'

He nodded. Inside himself he repeated the nod.

They finished the breakfast, had an extra coffee and a few cigarettes and then she walked him to the door. He put his hands on her face.

'You stay here,' he said. 'Wait for my call. I'll come back a little past noon and we'll drive out to see our estate.'

Her eyes were closed. 'I know this is permanent. I know it—'

As he left the house, it seemed to him that he had no weight at all.

The cab let him out at Kensington and Allegheny and he decided to walk the seven blocks back to the Spot. He didn't feel like returning to the Spot. He had no desire to see the Spot, wishing there was some other place he could go. What he really wanted to do was hail another cab and drive back to Della. He moved toward the Spot with a drag in his legs, a frown that became deeper as he came closer to the emeralds and Dohmer and Baylock.

He walked into the Spot to hear Dohmer cursing the kitchen. 'Mice,' Dohmer was shouting. 'These damn mice.' Then Dohmer appeared from the kitchen and stared at him. 'Where you been all night.'

'With a woman. Baylock sleeping?'

'Dead,' Dohmer said. 'We played cards until four-thirty. I took him for near a hundred. We got a flock of mice in the kitchen.'

'Go upstairs and wake him up.'

'What's wrong?'

'Do I look wrong?'

'You bet your life you do,' Dohmer said. 'You look from the clouds. Someone stick a needle in you?'

Harbin didn't answer. He watched Dohmer climbing the stairs, and put a cigarette in his mouth and began to chew on it, then pulled it from between his teeth and shredded the tobacco onto the floor. From upstairs, Baylock protested whiningly that all he wanted from life was to be let alone, to be allowed to sleep and die.

They came down and Baylock took one look at him and said, quickly, anxiously, with a bit of a hiss. 'What happened? I bet something happened.'

'Stop it,' Harbin started to light the cigarette but it was a mess. He took another one, 'I'm out.'

Dohmer looked at Baylock and Baylock gazed at a wall. Baylock's head turned like the head of a puppet. His eyes came back to Harbin and he said, 'I knew right away.' His head went on turning, aiming toward Dohmer. 'I knew something happened.'

'Nothing except that I'm walking out,' Harbin said. 'Listen to it and take it or don't take it. But I found myself a woman last night. I'm going away with her. Today.'

'He's away,' Dohmer gasped. 'He's all away.'

Harbin nodded slowly. 'That's the only way, the only way to put it.'

Baylock scratched the side of his face. He looked at Harbin, looked away. 'I don't see how you can do it.'

'Easy,' Harbin said. 'With the legs. Right, foot, left foot and you're walking out.'

'No,' Baylock shook his head quickly. 'No, you can't do it.'

'You can't do it,' Dohmer told Harbin.

'For God's sake.'

'The woman,' Baylock asked. 'Who's this woman?'

'Just a woman,' Harbin said. 'That's all you get.'

'You hear this?' Baylock posed Dohmer. 'You hear it? He says that's all we get. No rundown, no listing, no nothing. Just a woman, and he's going away. Like that,' and Baylock snapped his fingers. And then turned to Harbin, 'How well do you think you know me? How well do you think you know him?' and he pointed toward Dohmer. 'You really believe we'll stand here and watch you walk out?' Then he started to laugh, sliced it hard, peered at Harbin as though his eyes looked through slits in a wall. 'You're so wrong, Nat. You're so wrong it's almost comical. We can't let you walk out.'

Harbin felt the floor under his feet. It began to sag just a little. He waited for it to get firm again. He said, 'Keep the thing technical.'

Baylock held his arms wide. 'It's a hundred per cent technical. If you walk out, there's a crack in the dam. The dam gets wider. The water starts coming in. Your own words, Nat. We're an organization. We're hot as a furnace in seven big cities and you know how many small towns. If they get Dohmer, it's ten to twenty. Same with Gladden. If I get caught, goodbye everybody. Makes me a three-time loser and that's twenty to forty at a minimum. Listen, Nat,' and Baylock crouched, his eyes almost closed. 'When I die, I want to die in the sunshine.'

Harbin waited a moment. Then he shook his head slowly. 'You haven't made your point.'

'My point is,' Baylock's voice held a slight tremor, 'the minute you walk out of here, you're on the debit side.'

'You think,' Harbin said, 'I'd play it filthy? You think I'd ever open my mouth?'

'I don't think so,' Dohmer spoke huskily. 'I'd bet a million to one against it. But all the same it remains a bet.' He resumed shaking his head. 'I don't want to make this kind of a bet.'

'Another thing,' Baylock said. 'What about your split of the haul?'

'I'll want that.' Harbin was taking his mind ahead of them. He felt no interest in his split of the haul but now the thing was becoming stud poker and he saw the need for manoeuvring himself out of the wedge they had created around him.

Baylock moved in. 'He wants his split of the haul. That's real nice.'

'What's not nice about it?' Harbin made his

voice a little louder. 'When you say my split, you mean my split. Don't I get it?'

'No,' Baylock was testing him, weighing him. It wasn't good testing. It wasn't sufficiently hidden. Baylock's face showed the testing and gave Harbin the formula for the next move.

Harbin walked across the room and sat down on a chair that looked sick. He gazed thoughtfully at the floor, 'You're a dog, Joe. You know that? You realize what a dog you are?'

'Look at me,' Baylock shouted. 'You see me trying to walk out?' Baylock worked his way toward Harbin, seeming to be pulled along on tracks. 'I'm willing to talk it over but you won't talk.' Baylock waited for talk and Harbin offered nothing, and eventually Baylock said, 'All we want is the reason. Something we can believe.' Then Baylock was away from the poker table. 'Give it to us, will you? If you give it to us, maybe we'll understand. We can't believe this thing with the woman, we want to know what it really is.'

Harbin had it now, seeing the closed card Baylock had displayed, and knowing fully that he sat alone at the table with all the winnings, because actually they weren't in a class with him, they couldn't begin to compete with him when it came to manipulating a situation. It was definite. Yet, underneath his expressionless face he was angry with them. They were forcing him into an area of deceit, actually urging him to lie. And he hated to lie. Even in the line of business with outsiders he felt unsanitary when he was lying. And now they had so arranged it that he had to give them a lie.

He said, 'If you really want it, I'll give it to you. I'd hoped you wouldn't make me say it, but the way it is, I guess I'll just have to tell you.' He figured it was time for a sigh, and then, while they stared and didn't breathe, 'There's big jobs I want to do, and you just don't fit in. You don't have what I need. You don't have it, that's all.'

The quiet that came then was a quiet with their shock in it, their dismay, their agony. Dohmer had a hand to the side of his face, and he was shaking his head and making odd little noises deep in his throat. Baylock began walking aimlessly around the room, trying to say something and unable to pull a sound from his mouth.

'I didn't want to say it,' Harbin said. 'You made me say it.'

Baylock leaned against a wall and gazed at empty air. 'We don't have what you need? We ain't first-rate?'

'That's the thing. It's the nerves, mostly. I saw it coming and I didn't want to believe it. You've been getting shaky, the two of you. And Gladden doesn't have the health. I saw it the other night. I was bothered by it. Bothered too much.'

Baylock turned to Dohmer. 'He means we ain't in his league.'

'I want to hit very big jobs,' Harbin told them. 'Triple the risk. Jobs where every move is high-class dancing, where even your toenails have to be in place. I need the best people I can get.'

'You got them already?' Baylock asked.

Harbin shook his head. 'I'm going out to look for them.'

The quiet came again, and finally Dohmer stood up and sounded an immense sigh with a grunt in it. 'If it's got to be this way, it's got to be this way.'

'One thing.' Harbin was moving toward the door. 'Be good to Gladden. Be real good to her.'

Now he had his back to them. The door came closer. He heard Dohmer's heavy breathing. He thought he heard Dohmer gasping, 'Nat, for God's sake—' and a final pleading whimper from Baylock, and then another voice, and a shudder went through him as he sensed it was Gladden's voice. All their voices were with him as he opened the door, then floated away behind him as he walked out.

CHAPTER VII

Della's car was a pale green Pontiac, a new convertible, and they had the top down as they ran past Lancaster, going west on Route 30, holding it at fifty miles an hour with the sun over their heads and honeysuckle coming into their faces. The road dipped evenly, the hills rising smoothly, softly on both sides of the road. Then the road followed the lines of the hills and they were climbing.

'I notice,' Della said, 'you didn't bring your things.' She indicated his attire. 'Those all the clothes you have?'

'They're all I need.'

'I don't like the suit.'

'You'll get me another one.'

'I'll get you everything.' She smiled. 'What do you want?'

'Nothing.'

The Pontiac curved and climbed and reached

the top of a hill from where they looked out ahead, saw more hills, higher than this one, green hills a quiet glimmer under the heavy sun. A snake made of silver curled its way around one of the hills and as it came closer he knew it was the hill she had talked of, and the house was on that hill. He could see it now, a house of white stone and a yellow gabled roof, set on the slight plateau that interrupted the rise of the hill, and the silver snake was the brook, and now the pond, another thing of silver, and the river down and away to the north, and the lavender mountains.

She drove the car down, went up and down a few more hills, turned it onto a narrow unpaved road and again the car began to climb. They were going up the hill. Alongside, maybe fifty yards away, the brook going down from the pond to the river seemed to be climbing with them. He had a feeling they were going away from all the people of the world. There was another road, narrower than this one, and tall grass and trees came up and crowded them for a while, and then the house was there. She parked the car beside the house, and they got out of the car and stood there looking at the house.

'I bought it four months ago,' she told him. 'I've been coming up here weekends, staying here alone, wanting someone to be here with me. In this place. Here, completely here, and never to go away.'

They entered the house. She had done it in mostly tan, the colour of her hair, with yellow here and there, and a tan broadloom rug that stopped only when it reached the yellow kitchen. From the kitchen they could see the barn, the same oyster-white as the house. Then the rest of the small plateau that was a green table-top beyond the barn.

She seated herself at the piano and played something from Schumann. He stood near the piano. For a while he heard the music, but gradually it became nothing. He felt the frown cutting into his brow. Then he heard the abrupt quiet that meant her fingers were off the keys.

'Now,' she said. 'Now start telling me.'

He put a cigarette in his mouth, took a bite at it, took it out of his mouth and placed it carefully in a large glass ashtray. 'I'm a crook.'

After awhile she said, 'What kind?'

'Burglar.'

'Work alone?'

'I had three people with me.'

'What about them?'

'This morning I said goodbye.'

'They argue?'

'A little. I had to make it fancy. I said I had big plans and they didn't rate high enough to be included.'

She crossed the room and settled herself in a tan chair. 'What's your speciality?'

'We went in for stones. Now they got themselves a haul in emeralds and they'll have to wait a long time before making it into money. But all that's away from where I am now. It's strictly yesterday.'

'But it still bothers you.'

'One part of it.'

'I want to know about that. We've got to clear up anything that bothers you. We're starting now, and I don't want a single thing to bother you.'

'One of us,' he said, 'was a girl.' Then he told her about Gladden, and Gladden's father, and all the years of it. 'She always wanted to get out, but drilled it into herself she would never get out unless I did. Now I'm out. And where is she?'

'That's a question.'

'Help me with this,' he was walking up and down. 'Driving out here, I kept thinking about her. I felt rotten about it and I still feel rotten. I wish I knew what to do.'

Della smiled dimly. 'You have a feeling for this girl—'

'It isn't that. She depends on me. I've been her father. I've been her older brother. There were times I went away but she knew I'd come back. Now she's in Atlantic City, and tonight at seven she'll call a phone number and there won't be any answer. That eats away at me. I don't think she'll be able to take it. I think she'll go to pieces. It's getting worse inside me and I feel real bad about it, I wish I knew what to do.'

She put the palms of her hands together, took them away, put them together again. 'We'll have something to eat and then we'll start driving back to Philadelphia. You'll take that call at seven. Then I'll come back here. And I'll come alone.'

'No.'

'Mean it when you say it. Say it again.'

'No.' He made the decision out loud. 'The hell with her, let her call, let the phone ring a thousand times. I'm clear of all that, I'm away from it. I'm here with you, and that's all.'

Yet deep in the night he came halfway out of sleep and on the black of the ceiling he saw Gladden. He saw her walking alone on the boardwalk in Atlantic City, the black of the beach and ocean and sky all a black curtain, her yellow hair a vague yellow, her skinny body vague and seeming to float.

Blindly, to get away from Gladden, he reached for Della. His body twisted, almost lunging as his arms swept across the wide bed. But there was nothing under the blanket. Della wasn't there.

He sat up in the bed. She wasn't there. He was coming awake very quickly now, and his brain went into gear and told him to be quiet and accurate.

Enough moonlight came into the room to let him know where he was going. Invisible ropes pulled him across the room to the door. A new and unreasonable feeling came into his spine and his stomach and his brain. He had no idea what it was, only that it pumped away at him and caused him to stand motionless for a moment, facing the dark door, visualizing the hall beyond in terms of something bleak and grim.

He decided to use a method he had used many times in the past when there was an abundance of jeopardy. The method was simple. It was a matter of swerving his mind from night to day, forcing himself to see sunlight rather than darkness. He imagined it was broad daylight, and he was going out in the hall to call Della.

Opening the door, he stepped out in the hall. The bathroom door was wide open and the bathroom was dark. She wasn't upstairs. He wondered what she was doing downstairs. He knew now what the pumping was, this thing he was feeling for the first time in his life. It was the beginning of regret.

He returned to the bedroom, and groped for his clothes. He didn't realize the pumping was beginning to fade. It didn't occur to him he was riding away from himself, that the thing was becoming a project and now his moves were all arithmetic as they were when he was on a job. The moves were slow, precise, each move, even the tying of his shoelaces, a separate step in a series of steps carefully arranged.

He was in the hall again, moving down the hall toward the stairway. Downstairs it was dark. Midway down the stairs he waited, listened for a sound, any sound at all. There was no sound. There was no light down there. Instead of thinking now, he was calculating. The sum of it came easily. She was not in the house. He headed for the kitchen.

In the kitchen, his hand worked the doorknob as though it were an instrument that had to be worked with pure silence or not at all. There was no sound as he opened the door, and no sound as he stepped outside. The smell of the night was a smell of field and hill and tree, thick with springtime and flowers in the night.

He moved across grass, toward the white shape of the barn, then out away from the barn, coming back toward the house but staying wide of it to see what else there was to see. He saw the Pontiac parked beside the house. Then he saw something else, two things that moved. They moved just a little, near the trees that bordered the far side of the pond. He made them out as human figures, and one of them was feminine, and he knew it was Della.

Instead of focusing on Della, he centred his attention on the other figure, the man. The man was in silhouette and stood close to Della and it grew evident that they were in deep and urgent discussion. Then, as Harbin watched, the man and Della became a single silhouette, and they were in each other's arms.

They retained the embrace for several moments. When they broke it, the conversation was resumed. Harbin decided on the trees. He saw that he could circle around behind the barn to bring himself in on the far side of the trees on that side of the pond. Once in among the trees, he could wriggle in toward them and get close enough to hear what they were saying.

He did it that way, and began getting words, then phrases, then all of it.

'—in a couple of days.'

'It ought to be sooner than that,' the man said.

'Let's not be in too much of a hurry.'

The man said, 'Why don't we do this my way?'

'Because your way is wrong; now look, let's cut it out.'

'I don't want to cut it out. I want to talk about it. God damn it, a thing like this we should talk about. It's a big thing. You know what a big thing it is. I want to be sure it's handled right.'

Della said, 'It will be.'

'When should we make it?'

'Saturday,' Della said. 'At three in the afternoon.'

The man's voice became a bit louder. 'By Saturday night we ought to have it all wrapped up. Even then maybe it'll be too late. I still claim we're doing it too slow. If we did it my way, we'd be done by now.'

'You want to do it your way? You do it alone. I think that's a good idea. You better do it alone.'

'Did anyone ever tell you you're a nasty proposition?'

'I'm not at all nasty. I'm just certain. I'm certain of everything I do. If you haven't learned that by now, you better hurry and get wise to it.'

There was a long wait, and it ended with the man saying something so quietly that Harbin couldn't hear. Della answered in the same low tone. Harbin edged his face out from behind the tree and saw them embracing again. There was only one thing on his mind, and it was estimating. He estimated that they would keep on embracing long enough to allow him to get back into the house and undress and climb into the bed.

It took less than a minute. When he entered the bedroom he already had his coat and shirt off. He waited until he was in bed before sliding into his pyjamas. He worked his head into the pillow and closed his eyes. He felt the full feeling of having been lured, completely deceived.

It was like the in and out movement of a bellows that had been inserted in his flesh. He waited there in the bed with the pumping banging away at his insides, his brain trying to sit still but pulled around and around by the pumping. A few moments later the door opened and he heard her entering the room.

He listened as she moved around the room, felt her weight coming into the wide bed. But the weight didn't hit the bed fully. He sensed she was sitting there in the bed, looking at him.

Then, at the very instant when he wished he had the impetus to reach up and put his hands around her throat and choke the life out of her body, he felt her lips on his forehead. Not wanting to open his eyes, he opened his eyes. He murmured sleepily, and saw the shine of her lips and her eyes. Then her lips crashed into his mouth, and something lifted him high and hurled him out into space, his body speeding toward an unreal world.

CHAPTER VIII

In the morning, while she prepared breakfast, Harbin came back to himself, and began to figure his moves. The big thing he had to do was find out who the man was. But that would have to wait until Saturday. On Saturday, at three, she would meet the man and it would be in the afternoon, he would see the man in the daylight and know what the man looked like. That would gradually reduce the element of question and bring it toward an answer.

Until Saturday he realized, there was nothing for him to do but wait. In terms of clock time, it wasn't very long, but he knew this waiting would be an extremely difficult thing for him. He could already feel it, the impatience, the anxiety. Glancing at Della during breakfast, he saw her watching him. He told his face not to give him away. He knew it was these little things that could give him away. Like a sudden change of facial expression. Or a word in the wrong place.

In the afternoon they decided to take a long walk. She said it would be marvellous, walking through the hills. Maybe, she said, they would see some flowers they could collect. She was crazy about flowers she told him, especially wild flowers. She put on a sporty skirt and blouse and low-heeled shoes. They started on their walk. They moved past the barn, followed a path that took them toward the top of the hill.

They went for a walk the next day too, and Harbin kept on waiting for Saturday.

Saturday morning they slept late, didn't get to eat until around eleven. Della prepared a combination of breakfast and lunch. Afterwards, Harbin walked outside and strolled around, wondering what sort of pretext Della would use to get rid of him in the afternoon, and where and how she'd keep her appointment with the man.

A half hour later he found out. 'I have to run down to Lancaster,' she said. 'I want to do some shopping.'

Harbin knew that the next thing he said had to be said just right. 'When will you be back?' he said.

'Past five, anyway. Tons of things I've got to buy.'

He shook his head emphatically, showing a dim smile.

'I can't wait that long.'

It did what he wanted it to do. There was no way for her to answer. All she could do was copy his smile.

Then she said, 'You want to go with me?'

'Anywhere you go, I want to go with you.'

'Then you'll go with me. Except during the shopping. That's something a woman's got to do alone. I'll put you in a barber shop. You can stand a haircut.'

He said, 'You put me in a barber shop, you'll never get me out. Once I get in, I get the whole works. I stay there for hours.'

'Good,' she said. 'Because I've a lot of marketing to do.'

'I'll bet you do,' he said, without saying it aloud.

Later they climbed into the Pontiac and started toward Lancaster. Approaching the town, he said he could use a little money and she gave him close to a hundred dollars. She gave it to him without comment. He took it without comment. For the first time since leaving the Spot, he remembered that he had seven thousand dollars in small bills stashed away at the Spot. It didn't bother him. A few days ago, seven thousand dollars had been very important because it was all the money he had in actual cash. Now it was a minor detail.

They arrived in Lancaster at twenty after two. He said he could stand a few sport shirts, and waited for her to suggest that he choose his own store and pick them out himself. He waited for a trace of uneasiness in her voice, because she had less than forty minutes until her appointment with the man. Yet when she said she'd go with him to get the shirts, he wasn't at all surprised. It was already at the point where nothing she did surprised him.

It took a good half hour to buy the shirts. She did the selecting and the buying. When the package was wrapped and they were headed toward the door, she had less than ten minutes before her appointment with the man. She behaved as though she had all day. They passed a counter of neckties and Della stopped and looked at the ties.

She said, 'Like regimental stripes?'

'I go for polka dots.'

The salesman closed in and began to discuss the new styles. Della looked at the salesman as though he was peddling shoelaces. She said, 'I can't pick out these ties while you're talking.'

'Beg your pardon, Madam.' The salesman acted as though he had been given a good clout on the side of the head.

Harbin looked down at his wristwatch. Six minutes. He looked at Della. She was completely immersed in the subject of neckties.

'I'm not enthused about any of these,' she said. 'What else do you have?'

The salesman excused himself and went into a side room.

Della spent a good ten minutes selecting three neckties. Harbin could see the man at the meeting-place, maybe smoking one cigarette after another, or cracking the knuckles or biting the lips, waiting there for Della while Della was here, buying neckties.

Harbin said, 'I better get to the barber shop.'

'What's the hurry?'

The calm, easy way she said it threw a flag of warning against his eyes. He had displayed a touch of impatience, and with this woman, with this manipulator, he couldn't afford to display anything along that line.

He said, 'Saturday afternoon. They get busy

around three. I hate to sit around waiting.'

'Thank me for the neckties.'

'Thank you for the neckties.'

They were out of the store and she looked up and down the street, told him if they tried the next block they'd probably see a barber shop. They tried the next block and there was a barber shop near the far corner, but when they arrived there, Della said she didn't like the looks of it. Harbin studied his wristwatch. It was now twenty-two minutes past three.

'What's wrong with this place?' he asked. 'It looks clean.'

'The barbers look stupid.'

'Let's spend the day hunting for intelligent-looking barbers.'

It was another five minutes before they found the barber shop on Orange Street. Harbin smiled at Della and then he threw another look at his wristwatch. This time he let her know he was looking at it. He said, 'Where do we want to meet? What time?'

She peered through the big windows of the barber shop, a big clean shop with many chairs. 'There's four ahead of you. You're good for an hour and a half, at least. Wait here for me.'

He entered the shop, turning in time to see her headed in the direction from which they had come. It would take her twenty seconds at the minimum to reach the corner at the end of the block. He had to get outside to see whether she would turn the corner. He counted up to eight and then moved out of the shop and saw her turning the corner, going right. He crossed the street, walked fast to the corner, arrived there in time to see her turning another corner.

There was a crowd further ahead, and still another coming out of a department store across the wide street that Della had just crossed. Della was entering the department store. Harbin bumped into a trio of old women and almost knocked them down. They wanted to discuss it with him but he was already in the middle of the street, travelling against the light, racing the people who were aiming at the revolving doors of the big store. He beat them to the door, but going through it he could see the maze of people in the store and he knew he had lost her. He started to chew on the cigarette. An aisle said lingerie and another aisle said luggage and a third said toiletries. He selected luggage and halfway down the aisle he saw her among a flock of women waiting at the elevators.

Wondering how many floors this place had, telling himself he should have thought of that before, he stopped and turned his back on the elevators, and kept on chewing at the cigarette as he realized it was now necessary to gamble on what floor she would call.

It was difficult to let the seconds go by. He let fifteen of them pass before turning to face the elevators. She had already gone up. He took his time walking to the elevators. One of them arrived and opened for him, and he went in with a crowd of women and children. The coloured girl took the elevator to the second floor and called out furniture, rugs, radios, household essentials. At the third floor the coloured girl called sporting goods and men's wear, and Harbin got out. He told himself it was a fairly good bet, a basic thing. A reasonable place for the man to wait would be in the men's wear department.

It was rather crowded, and they were mostly boys and young men in this section that had the baseball bats and gloves, the tennis racquets and swimming trunks. He moved slowly, and a salesman walked towards him and he smiled easily, shook his head, murmured something about just looking around. He was in there with the suits and slacks now, his head turning slowly this way, that way, and going toward windows as he manoeuvred to always stay behind a row of hanging suits but sufficiently away from the suits so he could get a reasonable view of that part of the room near the windows.

He went up and down past two long rows of suits. Then he saw Della. He saw the man. They stood a little away from one of the windows. The salesmen were leaving them alone. The man had his back to Harbin but not all the way. The man was about five-ten and had a heavy build, and was young and had thick blond hair, blonder than Harbin's, a wealth of blond hair combed straight but sort of loose.

Harbin lifted a sport jacket from its hanger and held it up in front of his face, going through the motions of taking it toward a window where he could see it in the light. He manoeuvred the jacket to keep it in front of his face as he went sliding in toward Della and the blond man. He was coming toward them from an angle.

He pulled the jacket slowly away from his face, as though the jacket was a curtain. A fuzzy sleeve went past his eyes. A sizzling fuse began eating itself away as Harbin told himself he had seen the face before, had seen it very recently, had seen that nose and mouth. And the eyes. The eyes were an unusual colour. Very pale blue with a bit of green. Aquamarine eyes. A couple of nights ago, two cops had questioned him about the car parked near the mansion. This was the young cop.

CHAPTER IX

As Harbin entered the barber shop, a man got up from one of the wire-backed chairs in response to the barber's beckoning finger. Harbin lowered himself into the wire-backed chair. He leaned back, closed his eyes, saw the mansion in the night and the car parked on the wide clean street north of the mansion, the police car, the aquamarine eyes of the young cop.

Now he had to take it from there. He began to take it, very slowly considering each item before buying it. He had to check his own moves in ratio with the moves of the young cop, the things they were doing at the same time, the things in the mind behind the aquamarine eyes. That mind had decided to come back alone and have another look at the parked car. Maybe the aquamarine eyes had seen the flashlight signals going across the lawn minutes before Harbin had appeared. Maybe it was something else. Whatever it was, the young cop had decided the older cop was a hindrance, and it was best to come back alone.

And so the blond man, no longer to be

considered a policeman, had come back alone and had placed the police car so he could not be seen. He had watched the parked Chevrolet. He had seen them coming from the mansion with their haul. He had watched the Chevrolet as it went into first gear. Maybe he had followed them without using his headlights. That maybe didn't last long. In Harbin's brain it became an emphatic yes. He remembered having examined the rear-view mirror and not seeing any headlights.

Without headlights, this blind man had followed the Chevrolet to the Spot. He had watched them entering the Spot with their haul. That was for certain and another thing for certain was the fact that he had gone back to the police station and reported nothing.

Harbin realized it was necessary to check on that, check with himself, his own conception of how certain people react to certain situations. The aquamarine eyes had seen the luxurious mansion, the token of great wealth, had decided it would be a big haul, had waited calmly for the report to come in. When the report came in, when the house sergeant put it down in the book, and the fact that it amounted to around a hundred thousand dollars in emeralds, the man aimed his eyes and his body and his brain at the hundred thousand dollars.

And now it was all quite clear to Harbin and he could see the rest of it as though he sat at a table and looked at tangible things set neatly before him. He saw the man walking around and thinking it over, deciding to play it carefully and with accuracy. A policeman would have gone after the burglars, but this man was a policeman only when he wore a uniform and moved in the company of other policemen. This man was a rather special sort of operator, loyal only to himself and what he wanted. And what he wanted was the emeralds. This man realized the emeralds were in the shabby Kensington house and the only way to get them out and into his own hands was by using another brain. The other brain was a woman named Della.

The man had made contact with Della. They must have taken turns, keeping their eyes on the Spot, the legs that walked out of the Spot and then returned and walked out again. They must have decided on a time, the initial forward move. And Della had seen him entering the restaurant that night, and that was it, that was the arrangement she needed. If that hadn't worked, she would have tried something else. But that had worked. It had worked beautifully. It had kept on working until now, but now it was all over.

Harbin saw a thick finger pointing at him. The barber was smiling, inviting him to the chair. He climbed into the chair and the barber gave him a shave and then a haircut and after that a shampoo and scalp massage and then went back to the face and put pink cream on the face and worked it in with the thick fingers and followed with a sunlamp treatment. A folded towel kept the light out of Harbin's eyes. In the black under the folded towel he could see the Spot, he could see their faces, the three in the organization when it ought to be four in the organization. He was in a great hurry to get back to the Spot.

The barber took the folded towel from Harbin's eyes and pushed a button that then lifted the chair electrically to sitting position. Harbin got off the chair and saw Della standing near the door.

They left the barber shop and walked back to the car. They drove out of Lancaster and pulled onto the road going back to the hill. Della worked the radio and got some light-opera music. She pushed the car at medium-speed, sat there behind the wheel with a relaxed smile on her face as she listened to the music. Without looking at Harbin she was communicating with him and once she reached out and let her fingers go into the hair at the back of his head. She gave his hair a little pull.

He poked around in his brain and wondered if it was possible to figure her out. He thought of her kisses. In his lifetime he had been kissed by enough women and had experienced a sufficient variety of kisses to know when there was real meaning in a kiss. Her kisses had the real meaning, and not only the fire, but the genuine material beyond the fire. If it hadn't been genuine he would have sensed it when it happened. This woman had immense feeling for him and he knew clearly it was far above ordinary craving and it was something that couldn't be put on like a mask is put on. It was pure in itself and it was entirely devoid of pretence or embroidery.

It was the true feeling that made the entire business of quaking paradox, because the one side of Della was drawn to him, melted into him, and the other side of Della was out to louse him up. Even now, knowing of her purpose, knowing she was out to get the emeralds, fully aware of her scheme, seeing the situation as a sort of arena with her on one side and himself on the other, he felt the magnetic pull, he realized his desire for Della, the depth of the desire and the knowledge it was permanent desire. He knew he wanted Della more than he had ever wanted anything. This was a solid problem, this woman, a thing he had to deal with, a trouble he had to blast apart. Because it was a threat, and since it aimed at the emeralds, it had to aim at the Spot. And the Spot was the organization. The Spot was Dohmer and Baylock and Gladden. And there, right there, the quiver went through him, the edge of the knife sliced everything else away. This thing was aiming at Gladden.

Not knowing it, he had his eyes dulled and heavy with guilt. There was hammering in the guilt and it sent the heaviness through his veins. Every thread in his body became a wire drawn tight. Gladden needed him and he had deserted Gladden. Here he was, sitting at the very side of this thing that aimed a threat at Gladden. For days he had been with this thing, away from Gladden. Gladden needed him and if he wasn't there it would be the end of her. This woman sitting beside him was an element that he must quickly erase.

He glanced around at the hills, the woods beyond the hills. There were some narrow hills going to left and right of the concrete highway, and he said, 'Let's try some new scenery.'

She gave him a look. 'Where?'

'One of these little roads.' He said it with his eyes going into her, the words nothing more than ripples on the surface.

It worked. She nodded slowly. 'All right, we'll find a quiet place. Where we'll have a lot of trees around us. Like a curtain.'

They took one of the little roads, followed it up along a hillside, went up and around and down to the other side of the hill, followed the road into the woods where it became a set of tyre tracks. They were going far into the woods and the path became dim. Harbin glanced over the side of the car and watched the thick high green grass sliding along, some purple sliding with the green.

He felt the car slowing down and he said, 'No, keep going.'

'It's wonderful here.'

'Keep going.'

'Put your hand on me.'

'Wait,' he said.

'I can't.'

'Please wait.'

The woods around them were thick and up ahead it seemed to be thicker, very dark because the leaves were mobs of solid green high in the trees and holding the sun away. He knew she would say nothing new until he said something and he remained quiet while they went on through the woods. They went deeper and deeper into the woods and through an hour and through another hour, the car going very slowly because it was bumpy ground and there was considerable climbing and turning. He felt the immense yet gentle pressure of the woods and he felt the nearness of Della and for moments that choked him he was pulled away from his idea, his purpose, the thing he meant to carry out in these woods. He took hold of the moment and twisted it away from himself.

He said, 'All right. Just about here.'

She stopped the car. She turned off the radio.

He said, 'Get rid of the lights.'

She switched off the headlights and he opened the door on his side and stepped out of the car. Moonlight came down through the woods. Della was getting out of the car, circling it to come toward him. Her body came toward him through the moonlight. As she reached him he took her hand, he walked her away from the car, off the path, heard the sound of her breathing as he took her into the trees.

He took her on toward the rippling sound of water. Eventually they could see the water, the glimmer of a brook far down below from where they stood on a high mound of wild flowers.

He took her down to the brook and they stood there looking at the moon-glazed water, the points of rocks showing like bits of crystal against the dark. He lowered himself to the ground, felt the smooth flatness of it here on the bank, felt Della as she came against him. He sensed the approach of her lips. He drew his face away from her lips.

'No,' he said. He said it tenderly, almost like a caress, and yet he knew it had the force of a spear going into her.

He waited. He wanted to look at her, he wanted to see the effect, but this was only the start of what he was going to do to her, only an ounce of the full measure aiming at this thing that aimed the threatening aim in a long line going up from the emeralds to the Spot to the organization, and to Gladden. Inside himself he spoke softly to Gladden and told her he was about to make up for what he had done.

Della was quiet for many moments. Finally she said, 'What bothers you?'

'Nothing.'

'You don't seem to be with me.'

'I'm not.' He was smiling at the brook. He knew she could see the smile and he knew what it was doing to her.

There was another long wait and then she said, 'I know what this is.'

He went on smiling at the brook.

'You're drifting,' she said. 'I can see you drifting.'

He shrugged. ‘I imagine so.’

She stood up, had her back to him but he knew what was happening on her face. He could almost see inside her, see the tumult, the piercing shock, the agony she didn’t want him to see. She was trying to hold back but couldn’t hold back because finally it broke away and came out, bursting, hissing, her body twisting to show him her face as she said, ‘God damn you, you dirty son of a bitch.’

He looked at her only for an instant, then swerved his eyes to the brook and went on smiling at it.

‘Why?’ She shot it at him. ‘Why? Why?’

He shrugged.

‘You tell me why,’ she gasped, her voice almost cracking. ‘You better tell me why.’

The smile on his face became dim but inside himself he was smiling widely because this was the way he had planned it and it was working just right. He thought of certain people who had it in for some other people and went ahead and did their killing. But there was never any real benefit to be derived from killing, and the results, sooner or later, were always bad. So it was always stupid and crazy to kill, and this was so much more effective than killing. This was the worst possible thing he could do to her. It was the worst thing any man could do to any woman. It was the meanest form of torture, because he was rejecting her without qualifying the rejection, throwing her into a gully of dismay, watching her flounder and choke, her brain seething, trying to reach the reason while he held the reason just a trifle out of her reach.

He stood up. 'Guess that's about it.'

'You can't' she said. 'How can you? How can you do this? It isn't human. It's what a devil would do. At least give a person a reason, let me know why—'

'Why?' He made a little gesture with his arms. 'Go ask the trees. They know as much about it as I do.'

'I don't believe that.'

'I'm sorry.'

'You're not sorry. If you were, you'd tell me. You'd tell me what goes on in that mind of yours. What thoughts are you having? What are your feelings?'

'I don't know.' He said it as though she had asked him what time it was. Then, as he began to turn away from her, 'I don't know anything about it except I just don't want to be around you anymore. I want to get away.'

And as he moved away, as he went up the steep rise going away from the brook and into the woods, he could hear no sound beside him other than the sound of the water against rocks.

Moving steadily through the woods, seeing the car, he crossed the moonlit path far in front of the car and followed a stretch of a climbing terrain to get up high enough so he could obtain a view of the main highway, and started down in that direction.

On the highway, about an hour later, a truck picked him up and took him into Lancaster. He climbed into a taxi and went to the railroad station and bought a ticket to Philadelphia.

CHAPTER X

Opening the door, he saw only darkness. He called Baylock's name, then he called Dohmer. A weak light came down from upstairs, and he heard their voices. He switched on a lamp, took out a handkerchief and wiped some rain from his face. He waited for them to come down the stairs.

They came down rather slowly, looking at him as though they had never seen him before. They were both dressed, but their trousers were rumpled and he knew they had been sleeping in their clothes. They moved down into the living-room and stood close together, looking at him.

He opened his mouth. Instead of words coming out, a lot of air and worry rushed in. He didn't know how to begin.

They waited for him to say something.

Finally he said, 'Where's Gladden?'

They let him wait. He asked it again and then Dohmer answered, 'Atlantic City.'

He put a cigarette in his mouth. 'I guess I figured she'd come back here.'

'She did come back,' Dohmer said. 'We told her about you, so she went back to Atlantic City.'

Harbin took off his wet jacket and hung it on a chair. 'You talk as though she's gone for good.'

'You hit it,' Baylock said.

'Don't lie,' Harbin moved quickly toward them, caught himself and told himself to handle it another way. His voice was calm. 'What happened with Gladden?'

'We tell you she's pulled out,' Baylock said. 'She packed her things and pulled out. You want to make sure? Go to Atlantic City.' Baylock dipped a hand in his trousers pocket, took out a folded slip of paper and handed it to Harbin. 'Here's the address she gave us.' Baylock took a deep breath that had grinding in it. 'Anything else you want?'

'I want you to listen while I talk.'

He studied their faces for a sign of trust. There was no sign. There was nothing.

He said, 'I want to come in again.'

'You won't come in,' Baylock told him. 'You're out. You'll stay out.'

'I'll come in,' Harbin said. 'I've got to come in because if I don't, you stand a good chance of losing the haul and getting yourselves grabbed. Now, either show some sense and listen to me or you'll wind up in a mud puddle.'

Baylock looked at Dohmer. 'I like how he walks back in and right away he takes over.'

'I'm not taking over,' Harbin said. 'All I can do is tell you the way things are shaped. We've got ourselves a package of grief.' He let that come against them, waiting until it went into them, and then giving it to them. 'We're being looked at.'

They moved in no special direction. They stared at each other and then they stared at Harbin. For a moment he was with them, he felt what they felt. He wanted to come out and put the whole thing in front of them, the thing as it had happened and the way it was. But he realized they wouldn't accept the truth. They hadn't accepted it the last time and they wouldn't accept it now. He would have to slice most of it away and give them nothing more than a mouthful to chew on.

He said, 'A party's been trailing me. It took me four days to find out. Another day to shake him. But I've added it up and I can see that shaking him won't do any good. At least not for the time being. Anyway, not until we get out of here.'

Baylock took another deep breath. 'Be careful, Nat. We got a lot more brains now than the day you walked out. We been educating ourselves.' He grinned at Dohmer. 'Ain't we?'

'Yeah,' Dohmer said. 'We took it serious, what you said, Nat. We made up our minds to get smarter. Now we're smarter and we're not nervous like we were.'

'Try to follow it.' Harbin was begging himself to stay away from anger, to hold on, to keep it cool. 'At the mansion we had the police. When they went away I thought for sure that was the end of them. But one of them came back. He followed us here. And now, in plain clothes, he's been following me.'

Baylock held onto the grin and shook his head. 'No fit. When they want you, they don't follow you. They move in and grab you.'

'The point is,' Harbin said, 'he doesn't want me.' Harbin let some quiet come in, let it settle. 'All right, if you can't figure it out, I'll tell you. The man stays with me but he doesn't want me. He wants the emeralds.'

Baylock turned and stopped, turned again, came back to where he had been standing. Dohmer lifted a hand and rubbed a long, heavy jaw. Then Baylock and Dohmer frowned at each other and that was all they could do.

Baylock said, breathing very heavily, 'Who is he? Who is this bastard?'

'I don't know. All I know is, the man is hungry for emeralds. He's got his police uniform to fall back on and when it lines up like that, the only way to deal with them is stay away from them.'

'But maybe,' Dohmer blurted, 'all he wants is a cut.'

Harbin shrugged. 'They all want just a little cut. To begin with. Then they come back and say they want another little cut. Then later they're back again.' He lit a cigarette, took several small puffs at it, blew out the smoke in one big cloud. 'What we've got to do and do fast is get the hell out of here.'

'Where to?' Dohmer said.

Harbin looked at him as though it was a silly question. 'You know where. Atlantic City.'

'For God's sake,' Dohmer groaned.

Baylock said, 'If she's pulled out, she's pulled out.'

'No,' Harbin said. 'We go there and pick her up.'

'Answer me this,' Baylock shouted. 'What do we need her for?'

'We don't need her,' Harbin admitted. 'But she needs us.'

'Why?' Baylock wanted to know.

'We're an organization.' Harbin knew he shouldn't have said that, but it was said and all he could do was wait for Baylock's blast.

'Are we?' Baylock shouted. 'Jesus Christ, give us credit for half a brain anyway. You walk out of here and say you're through and now almost a week later you show up again and once more we're an organization, just like that. I don't like it handled that way and I won't see it handled that way. Either it's black or it's white. One or the other.'

'I won't argue,' Harbin said. 'If you want to break it up we can break it up here and now. On the other hand we can hold it. And if we hold it, I stick. We all stick. That includes Gladden.'

Dohmer hit his hand against his thighs. 'I'm with that.'

'You're with everything.' Baylock looked Dohmer up and down. He turned his face to Harbin. He started to say something and then his mouth tightened up and he walked to the window and looked out at the rain.

The rain was coming down very hard, pouring off the rooftops in solid sheets of silver water against the black. Baylock stood there looking at the rain and hearing the thud of it and saying, 'It sure is a fine night to ride down to Atlantic City.'

Harbin made no reply. He started up the stairs, then stopped and looked at Dohmer. 'I'll do the driving. I hope you got the cards printed.'

Dohmer took out his wallet and extracted a few cards, including an operator's licence, a registration card, and a social security card and handed these to Harbin. He examined them, saw that the alias was neither far-fetched nor too common, then he beckoned to Dohmer and Baylock. The three of them went upstairs and packed their bags. They loaded the emeralds into a ragged suitcase, picked up their luggage and moved slowly out of the Spot and walked through the rain.

The Chevrolet was parked in a nearby one-car garage they had rented from an old couple who didn't have a car and were out of touch with the world. Dohmer had made the necessary changes so that now the Chevrolet was a darkish orange and had different licence plates, a different engine number and looked altogether like a different car.

Harbin drove and Baylock sat beside him. Dohmer was in the back and sound asleep before they hit the Delaware Bridge. There were very few cars on the Bridge. When they had driven halfway across the Bridge, Baylock began to worry.

'Why did we have to paint it orange?' Baylock wanted to know. 'Of all the colours we could have used, we had to use orange. Some colour for a car. Who paints a car orange?'

'You're worrying about the law,' Harbin said, 'and our worry right now is not the law.'

'Another thing,' Baylock said. 'Why in Christ's name did we have to take the car anyway? Why didn't we grab a train?'

'And put the emeralds on a train. And being there on a train going eighty miles an hour and not being able to get off if something goes wrong. If you want to make talk, let's make talk with sense.'

The car reached the New Jersey side of the river and Harbin paid New Jersey twenty cents for the use of the Bridge. In Camden the rain died down a little. Coming onto the Black Horse Pike the rain started again. It grew to become a wide rain with a great deal of Atlantic

Ocean wind in it.

Harbin worked the car up to fifty-five and held it there on the wet black road. The rain was seemingly coming straight at the car and he had to bend over a little, getting his eyes closer to the windshield to see where he was going.

Baylock said, 'Gladden looked good.'

'What do you mean, she looked good.'

'Her face. She looked good in the face. She had some colour.'

'The salt air,' Harbin said. 'It's good for everybody. The salt air and the sun.'

'It wasn't sunburn,' Baylock sounded emphatic. 'And where does salt air affect the eyes? I took one look at her and right away I noticed the eyes.'

'What's wrong with her eyes?'

'Nothing. Her eyes look great. I never saw her eyes like that before. I guess that's what happens to the eyes in Atlantic City. They get that real Atlantic City look. She sure was anxious to get back. As if there was something there that she was lonesome for. Like the salt air. And the sunshine.'

'All right,' Harbin said.

'And so,' Baylock said, 'the thing I keep asking myself is why we're going to all this trouble, going down there to Atlantic City to take her away from what she wants.'

Harbin couldn't form a reply, He had his mind completely on the road and the fight he had to make against this attack of northeaster wind and rain.

'All this trouble,' Baylock suddenly whined. 'And all this risk.'

'Quit harping on the risk.' Harbin was annoyed. 'There's no risk. Why don't you rest your head back and take a nap?'

'Who can sleep in this weather? Look at this God damn weather.'

'It'll let down.' Harbin knew the storm wouldn't let down. It was getting worse, there was more rain, heavier wind, and now he had to keep the car down to forty, and even at that speed he had difficulty hanging on to it.

'I'll make book,' Baylock said, 'we're the only car tonight on the Black Horse Pike.'

'That's a safe bet.'

'Even the cats,' Baylock whined, 'stay home on a night like this.'

Harbin was about to say something, but just then the car hit a chughole in the road and there was a nasty sound as the rear springs strained to keep themselves alive. The car went down and up and down again, and Harbin waited for it to fall apart. It went on riding through the northeaster. The headlights found a road sign that said Atlantic City was forty-five miles away. Then the road sign was past them and in front of them was the black and the booming storm. Harbin had an odd feeling they were a thousand miles away from Atlantic City and a thousand miles away from anywhere. He tried to convince himself the Black Horse Pike was a real thing and in daylight it was just another concrete road. But ahead of him now it looked unreal, like a path arranged for unreal travel, its glimmer unreal, black of it unreal with the wet wild thickness all around it.

Baylock's voice came to him, the whine of it cutting through all the clashing noise of the storm. 'I know for sure now,' Baylock said, 'we made a big mistake. We were crazy to start this. I can't tell you how sorry I am we started it. And while we still got the chance we got, we better junk off this road.'

'We'll get there.' Harbin knew it was a stupid thing to say. It signified he was trying to reassure himself, as well as Baylock.

And Baylock said, 'You're always the brains and we're always the goats. But now I'm wondering after all how much brains you really got. This party who trailed you, maybe he's the big brains. So let's see how his brains would work. Enough brains to find the Spot. Enough to keep checking on us. Here's a maybe for you. Maybe he trailed Dohmer, too. Maybe he trailed Dohmer to the garage and watched Dohmer painting the car.'

'You sound like you're from nowhere. Drop it.'

'It just can't be dropped. You grab hold of high voltage, you can't let go. This party, like you claim, is after the emeralds, not us. That fits. But here's another thing. If he loses us, he loses the emeralds. So now we've got to think of it the way he would think of it. Even though he ain't with the law, he can still give the law enough inside dope to make sure we don't break away.'

'You tell me how he could manage that.'

'Why should I have to tell you? You ought to know yourself. You're an expert on everything. And even a dumbbell can figure what the man does. He puts in a call to the station house, and he's anonymous, and he makes a few statements about an orange Chevrolet. Says it's a dark orange and has a lot of fancy chrome. Says nothing about the emeralds or the haul, just says it's a stolen car.'

'Come out of the trees.'

'You're in the trees. You're trying to dodge away from it but you know, just like I do.' Baylock's voice had climbed so that it was no longer a whine, but somewhere near a screech.

'You and your brain. You and your obligations. This skinny girl who needs Atlantic City. Who likes the colour orange. You and your girl Gladden.'

Harbin took the car up to forty. Then past forty. And then he took it up to fifty, and then to sixty. He felt the tremor of the car as he pushed it to seventy miles an hour through the bedlam of northeaster force and water. He heard every loud noise in the world bending to become one big banging noise, and through it he heard the wail of Baylock, though Baylock was begging him to slow down, then listened hard, knew the wail meant something else.

'I told you,' Baylock shrieked and wailed. 'You see? I told you.'

Baylock's fingers tapped the rear-view mirror, Baylock's hand shaking, his fingers on the mirror showing Harbin the two little spheres of bright yellow in the black mirror.

'It's nothing.' Harbin lessened his pressure on the accelerator. The two glowing spheres became just a bit larger, and he gave the car more gas. Again there was a wail, but almost instantly he knew it wasn't Baylock's wail. It was mechanical. He listened to it, studied it, and knew it was a police siren and it came from back there where the headlights sent their gleam into his rear-view mirror.

'Wake Dohmer,' he shouted. He looked at the speedometer. The car was holding seventy. He heard Dohmer grumbling, coming out of sleep, and then the clash between Dohmer's voice and Baylock's voice. From the corner of his eye he saw Baylock opening the glove compartment, reaching in deep to open another compartment that had been built by Dohmer for the concealment of revolvers. He saw the flash of the gun barrels as Baylock took them out. Dohmer in the back seat was bumping around like a big animal, twisting to look through the rear window.

'Put the guns back,' Harbin said.

Baylock was checking the guns, making sure they held slugs. 'Quit kidding yourself.' Baylock hefted the guns.

'Put them back,' Harbin said. 'We've never used them before and we won't need to use them now.'

'You better be damn certain about that.'

'I am. Put them back.'

'For God's sake,' Dohmer shouted. 'Go faster, will you? For God's sake, what in God's name is happening here? Why don't you go faster? What are you slowing down for?'

The car was down to sixty. It kept slowing down and the two dots of light in the rear-view mirror became larger. Harbin turned his face a little toward Baylock.

'I want you to put the guns back,' Harbin said.

The siren wail of the police car came biting through the northeaster, getting the fire of its drastic sound into Harbin's head, burning there in his head as he kept telling Baylock to put the guns back and close the contrived compartment.

Baylock said, 'I know we need guns.'

'You start with guns and you're dead.'

'We're using the guns.'

Harbin had the car down to forty miles an hour. 'I won't tell you again,' he said, 'put them back.'

'You sure you want me to do that?'

'I couldn't be more sure.' Harbin said.

He saw the flash again as the guns went back into the glove compartment. Baylock's arm deep in there getting the guns into the space on the side, and he heard the click as the side panel closed. Now he could no longer hear the police siren. From back there they could see he had slowed down and would be waiting for them to come up. The Chevrolet faded from thirty down to twenty, down to fifteen, and then it stopped altogether at the side of the road.

Harbin wondered whether it would be a good

thing at this point to light a cigarette. In front of him the rain washed down across the wearily sliding windshield wipers, more rain washed down and through the black beyond that, and more rain beyond that. He put a cigarette in his mouth and leaned his head back as he lit the cigarette. Now he could hear the engine of the police car coming up, and there was the floating wide swath of its headlights making bright white designs on the ceiling of the Chevrolet. There was something else he heard, and when he saw it happening it was already too late, he couldn't stop Baylock now, he couldn't close the glove compartment to catch Baylock's hand. Baylock already had the gun and was holding it close to his side as the police car pulled up alongside the Chevrolet, and Harbin twisted his head to stare at Dohmer. He saw Dohmer nodding slowly and knew that Baylock had manoeuvred it quickly and nicely and Dohmer had the other gun.

'Don't use them,' Harbin said. 'I'm begging you not to use them.'

He didn't have time to say anything else. A big man wearing a hooded raincoat had stepped out of the police car, the spotlight of the police car shooting past Harbin's face and giving enough light to brighten up the entire area and display the other two police faces in the official car.

Harbin lowered the window and let some smoke come out of his mouth. He saw the big shiny face of the big policeman, very shiny and weird in the mixture of light and rain.

'What's the big hurry?' the policeman said. 'You know what you were hitting?'

'Seventy.'

'That's twenty too much,' the policeman said. 'Licence and owner's card.'

Harbin took the cards from his wallet and gave them to the policeman. The policeman was studying the cards but made no move to pull out his book.

'We people in Jersey want to stay alive,' the policeman said. 'You drivers from Pennsylvania come over here and try to kill us.'

'You see what kind of a night it is,' Harbin argued. 'We only wanted to get out of this weather.'

'Call that an excuse? That's all the more reason to stay inside the speed limit. And you were doing something else, too. Crossing over the white line. You were way over on the wrong side of the road.'

'The wind kept pushing me over.'

'The wind had nothing to do with it,' the policeman said. 'If you're a careful driver and obey the law you don't have to worry about the wind.' He turned to the other policemen. 'I told you he'd blame it on the storm.'

'Well,' Harbin sighed, 'I know I've seen better weather than this.'

'You going down the shore?'

Harbin nodded.

The policeman said, 'You want nice weather, you won't find it in Atlantic City. Not for the next day or so, anyway. And I tell you, I wouldn't want to be down there tonight. When that ocean gets it from the northeast, there's no worse place to be.'

He handed the cards back to Harbin and Harbin put them in the wallet. The book had not appeared and Harbin told himself it was all right, it was over, and what remained wouldn't be important.

'Now, you be careful,' the policeman warned. 'Unless you're inclined to be a lunatic, you won't do more than forty miles an hour. Go into a skid on this road and you'll wind up in a grave.'

'I'll remember that, officer.'

The policeman turned to get back into the official car, and just then one of the other cops steered the spotlight so it would swish its wide glow into the Chevrolet, and the big policeman kept turning his eyes automatically to follow the path of the spotlight. The glow went riding past Harbin's head into the rear of the Chevrolet. Harbin pivoted his head, saw the glow catching Dohmer in the back seat, the revolver in Dohmer's hand in the middle of the glow. Then, as the big policeman let out a grunt and went for his own revolver, Dohmer raised the gun and pointed it at the big shiny face.

'No, don't, don't,' Harbin pleaded, but he heard the explosion of Dohmer's gun as the policeman went for his own gun. On the other side of the car Baylock already had the door open and was leaping out. Harbin tried to move and couldn't understand why it was impossible to move. He stared at the big policeman.

The face of the big policeman was completely destroyed, split wide open by the bullet and now sinking under the path of the spotlight. Harbin saw convulsive movement in the police car, sensed his own body moving, the backward rush as he threw himself toward the door that Baylock had opened. Falling out of the car, going backwards, he saw Dohmer leaping away toward a vague mass that was bush fringing the muddy ditch that fringed the road. He heard the crash of more bullets, heard the yelling of the policemen as they circled their car and came running toward the bush. They were running toward Dohmer and shooting at him as he sought to get inside the bush. Dohmer was more clumsy now than he had ever been before. He had managed to get past the ditch, but now he tripped with the bush coming up in front of him, got up and tripped again and fell into the bush and became entangled there. Then Dohmer knew he was due to be hit and he let out a scream, and right after that he was hit. He squirmed, his hands mixed with the bush. His body was an arc as he threw his shoulders far back. The policemen ran in close to him and shot him again as he twisted to give them his face and his stomach. They shot their bullets into his stomach. He screamed at the policemen. He screamed at the rain and the raining sky. He began to fall, but he was too clumsy to merely fall. He stumbled as he fell, and while stumbling he lifted his revolver and fired one and two and three shots at the policemen. One of the policemen died instantly, his heart pierced. The other policeman began to sob and let out a choking, gurgling noise as he clutched at his chest. Dohmer's body collided with him and they both went to the ground. The policeman pulled himself up and away from the corpse of Dohmer and crawled on his hands and knees toward the ditch, then rolled into the ditch.

Harbin, crouching at the side of the Chevrolet, waited for the policeman to climb out of the ditch. But all Harbin could see was the quiet legs of the policeman, coming from the top of the ditch. Then there was sound from another section of the bush, and Harbin turned to see Baylock emerging from the bush, Baylock following the line of bush toward the legs of the policeman. Harbin called to Baylock, and Baylock stopped, turned quickly, looked at him, then moved on toward the policeman. Now the legs were moving, the policeman was trying to pull himself from the muddy water. Baylock, his arm extended with the revolver at the end of the arm, walked up to the policeman, stared at him, aimed the revolver at him.

The revolver was only inches away from the policeman's head as Harbin came lunging towards Baylock, calling to him, pleading with him to forget the policeman and pull out of there. Again Baylock turned and looked at Harbin, motioned Harbin to stay away, then put two bullets in the policeman's skull.

Rain came showering into Harbin's eyes. He wiped the rain from his eyes and stood still and looked at Baylock. He had no thoughts about Baylock. He had no thoughts about anything or anyone in particular. He saw Baylock examining the bodies of Dohmer and the policemen. He followed Baylock toward the road and watched Baylock examining the body of the policeman who had been hit in the face.

'Get in the car,' Harbin said.

Baylock straightened himself, walked away from the Chevrolet and blindly opened the door of the police car and began to climb in.

'Not that car,' Harbin said.

Baylock turned. 'Where's our car? The car we got?'

'Right in front of you. You're looking at it.'

'I can't see it,' Baylock let out a cough, then a series of coughs. 'Let's go back to the Spot. Let's be at the Spot.'

Harbin walked over to Baylock and took him toward the Chevrolet and helped him get in. Then Harbin was behind the wheel of the Chevrolet, putting it in gear, taking it out onto the road, getting it in second gear, working it up fast, the transmission grinding hard as the car went into high gear. The tyres made a big splash through water that filled a hollow in the road. Then the water became higher further on up the road and they began running into a succession of lakes in the road. It seemed to Harbin that the interior of the car was a part of the lakes. The steering wheel felt like water. His body felt like it was all water.

'What are we doing?' Baylock asked.

'We're in the Chevrolet. We're going to Atlantic City.'

'I don't want to go there.'

'That's where we're going.'

'I want to go back to the Spot. That's the only place I want to go.'

'Where's your revolver?' Harbin wanted to know.

'Look at the rain. Look how it's raining.'

'What did you do with your revolver?' Harbin asked. 'Did you drop it?'

'I guess that's what I did,' Baylock said. 'I must have dropped it. We better go back there and get it.'

'What we better do,' Harbin was saying aloud to himself, 'is get off this road.'

'Let's get off this road and go back to the Spot.'

The road was level again and there were no more little lakes. Lights showed up ahead and Harbin could see it was one of the small towns that blotted the Black Horse Pike on its way to Atlantic City. He looked at his wristwatch and the hands read past two in the morning. It was too late to catch a bus or even a train. Their only way to get to Atlantic City was to stay in the car and take it onto a side road and keep it on the side roads away from the policemen who would soon be cluttering the Pike and stopping every car. He saw a road branching off to the right and knew it represented a chance. It might be a negative chance but he couldn't stop to think about that. The Chevrolet went onto the side road and followed it for a few miles, then cut onto another road that paralleled the Pike.

Baylock said, 'We're going the wrong way.'

'Why do you say that?'

'Because I know. We been making wrong turns.'

'You're crazy,' Harbin said.

Baylock said, 'We ought to have a gun.'

'We ought to have a lot of things. We ought to have a special apparatus that pulls back on your hand when you go for a gun.'

'I tell you,' Baylock insisted, 'what we need is a gun. If I hadn't dropped my gun back there I'd have it now. I can't begin to tell you how much I miss that gun.'

'If you don't shut up,' Harbin said, 'you'll go even crazier than you are now. And you're plenty crazy now. Why don't you shut up? Why don't you try to get some rest?'

'That's what I ought to do,' Baylock admitted. 'I ought to fall asleep. I'd feel a lot better if only I could sleep.'

'Give it a try.'

'Wake me up if anything happens.'

'If anything happens,' Harbin said, 'I won't have to wake you.'

He sent the Chevrolet onto a narrow road that aimed east. For the better part of an hour he followed the road, then had to turn where the road turned, going north. Instead of taking him toward Atlantic City, the road was pulling him away, but he had to follow the road and wait for it to start east again. He heard the heavy breathing of Baylock and every now and then Baylock mumbled something that had no meaning. A new atmosphere came into the car and it was the atmosphere of complete solitude, as though Baylock did not exist. Outside the car, the storm came sweeping in from the ocean. Now the road was sliced by another road that went east. Harbin made the turn. He listened to the rain and the bang and smash of the storm.

CHAPTER XI

Then, far out in the ocean, something unnatural took place with the northeaster and threw it acutely off its course. The waves that had been big and fast, dashing it on Atlantic

City, now began to calm down, and the rain became a light rain that lessened to a drizzle and toward four in the morning the storm was ended. It ended completely only a few minutes before the Chevrolet arrived in Atlantic City, the full thick black that meant soon it would start getting light, and Harbin took the car down a small street leading to the Bay. He parked the car at the end of the street, walked to the dock and saw a few cabin cruisers were bouncing lightly on the water. It seemed that here the water was deep enough for the purpose Harbin had in mind. He knew he had to do it before the sky lighted up. He walked to the car, got in, put the car in reverse and took it back up the street for thirty yards or so, then pulled the emergency brake and gave the sleeping Baylock an elbow in the side.

'You got the legs, Baby,' Baylock moaned. 'You got the wonderful kind of legs. Keep your dresses short so I can see your legs.'

'Come on, wake up,' Harbin said.

'Now see here, Baby, you—' Baylock blinked several times, opened his mouth, held it open and closed it hard, tasting his mouth and making a face at the taste of it. He sat up straight and rubbed his eyes. He looked at Harbin.

'We're here,' Harbin said. 'I'm throwing the

car in the Bay. Help me get the bags out.'

'What bay?'

'You'll see it. Let's do this fast.'

They took the bags from the car, all the bags except Dohmer's big brown suitcase. Then Harbin climbed into the car and put it in gear, driving it toward the Bay. He had the door open and he opened it wider as the car approached the water. The edge of the dock came up and he leaped out of the car and started running back toward the bags and Baylock. He heard the splash and hoped the water would be deep enough to cover the car, maybe even deep enough to hide it, but he didn't have time to go back and make sure. Approaching Baylock, he waved Baylock on. Baylock picked up the two smaller bags and began running, leaving Harbin one more small bag and the suitcase containing the emeralds.

They covered two long city blocks and were on the third when a cab cruised up the street. Baylock yelled to the cab and it stopped for them. They piled in with their bags. Harbin said he wanted a cheap hotel. The driver took a second look at Harbin's attire. Harbin, amiable, asked him what he was looking at, and he said he wasn't looking at anything special.

The cab pulled up in front of a miserable-looking place on a small street off Tennessee Avenue. Harbin paid the fare, tipped the driver a quarter and said he wished he could give more. The driver smiled good-naturedly, threw the cab in gear and drove it away.

They entered the hotel and the clerk took them up to a room on the second floor. It was a two-dollar double. It looked terrible. The window opened out on the wall of another building and Baylock said they would suffocate in here. Harbin said they wouldn't be here long enough to suffocate.

Baylock asked, 'How long we staying?'

'Until I get Gladden.'

'When you getting her?'

'Now.' Only he didn't feel like going now. He wanted the bed. He was very anxious about the bed. His muscles were tired, his arms, after all the arduous driving, were extremely tired. But worst of all were the eyes. His eyes wanted to close and he had to work hard to keep them from closing.

Harbin lit a cigarette, and walked out of the room. Downstairs in what they used for a lobby he saw a pay phone on the wall and mechanically he took from his coat pocket the folded paper on which was written the address of her hotel and the phone number. He wanted to call her, to tell her he was in town and would see her tomorrow. It would be more convenient to call. It would allow him to walk upstairs and fall into bed. He couldn't remember a time when he had been so tired. The pay phone invited him to start dialling, but he knew that phoning wouldn't be enough. He was deeply aware of the importance of going to her, being with her.

On Tennesse Avenue he walked toward the boardwalk. The sky was still black when he reached the boardwalk, but far out past the beach and the broken line of white breakers he saw the beginning of thin dawn above the ocean. The boardwalk, still wet, looked as though a corps of polishing experts had been at work on it for weeks. Every fourth lamp along the railing was dimly lit and that was the only light except for the faint push of dawn coming in from the ocean. With that, there was the heat, the unnatural heat that couldn't be coming from the ocean. It had to be coming from the meadows and swamps of New Jersey to the north of the seashore. Along the boardwalk the faces of the beachfront hotels were quiet and listless, waiting passively for the throngs who would come when summer arrived, merely tolerating the sprinkle of guests who now had the best rooms at off-season prices.

He looked back at what had happened on the Pike. It was an actual display of the law of averages. It had been bound to happen sooner or later. Something on the same order had happened once before, a long time ago in Detroit, the night when Gerald Gladden had made the pavement wet with the red coming out of his skull. That night had formed itself to a pattern, and it was being repeated tonight. Because that night, as he ran from the police, he had moved in a direction that took the little girl who was Gerald Gladden's daughter. And tonight the same thing was happening. He was moving toward Gerald Gladden's daughter, to lift her up and carry her away before anything bad could happen to her.

The pattern. And all these years, in modified ways, his every move had followed within the pattern. It was always necessary to get back to Gladden, to be with Gladden, to go with Gladden. It was more than habit and it was deeper than inclination. It was something on the order of a religion, or sublimating himself to a special drug. The root of everything was this throbbing need to take care of Gladden.

A contradiction came into it. He saw the contradiction coming in, beginning that night in the after-hour club when he had suggested to Gladden that she go to Atlantic City and get herself a bit of rest. The contradiction lengthened as he remembered Gladden's asking him to come with her and his saying no. It meant the pattern was beginning to fall apart, making him susceptible to the formation of another pattern and another drug and another religion or whatever in God's name had happened to him as he sat there in the restaurant and found himself being dragged across space by the woman's eyes.

Yet now he was back within the vague yet stern boundaries of the Gladden pattern. As he concentrated on it the vagueness gradually took on emphasis, like a wispy scene gradually brought into clear focus by the turning of a lens. He was digging through the reasons, digging through the layers of reasons for all the moves he had made since the afternoon when Gerald Gladden had found him sick and starving on a western road. He had been an infant, sixteen years old, with nothing in his mind but a drastic need for food, and the piteous bewilderment of an infant begging for aid from a world that wouldn't listen. Only Gerald had listened. Only Gerald had picked him up and given him food. It was stolen food because Gerald had paid for it with money gained from the sale of stolen goods. It was illegal food but it was food, and if he hadn't eaten it he would have died. Later, after their first job together, Gerald had explained this to him. Gerald liked to explain, not only about the tactics and science of burglary, but the philosophy behind it, anyway Gerald's philosophy. Gerald was always contending that burglary is no special field of endeavour, and every animal, including the human being, is a criminal, and every move in life is a part of the vast process of crime. What law, Gerald would ask, could control the need to take food and put it in the stomach? No law, Gerald would say, could erase the practice of taking. According to Gerald, the basic and primary moves in life amounted to nothing more than this business of taking, to take it and get away with it. A fish stole the eggs of another fish. A bird robbed another bird's nest. Among the gorillas, the clever thief became the king of the tribe. Among men, Gerald would say, the princes and kings and tycoons were the successful thieves, either big strong thieves or suave soft-spoken thieves who moved in from the rear. But thieves, Gerald would claim, all thieves, and more power to them if they could get away with it.

He had listened to Gerald because there was no one else to whom he could listen. There was no one else around. He had listened and he had believed. Gerald was the only external. Gerald's teachings were the only teachings. Gerald's arguments were not only forceful in delivery, they were backed with fact and qualified with history. Gerald's mother had been part Indian, her mother all Indian, all Navajo. For Christ's sake, Gerald would yell, take a look at how they robbed the Indians, and how they arranged a set of laws to justify the robbery. Always, when Gerald got himself started on the Navajo theme, he would go on for hours.

Gerald would say that aside from all this, aside from all the filthy dealing involved, the stink of deceit and lies and the lousy taste of conniving and corruption, it was possible for a human being to live in this world and be honourable within himself. To be honourable within oneself, Gerald would say, was the only thing could give living a true importance, an actual nobility. If a man decided to be a burglar and he became a burglar and made his hauls with smoothness and finesse, with accuracy and artistic finish, and got away with the haul, then he was, according to Gerald, an honourable man. But the haul had to be made correctly, and the risks had to be faced with calm and icy nerve, and if associates were involved, the associates had to be treated fairly, the negotiations with the fence had to be straight negotiations. There were categories of burglars just as there were categories of bankers and meat-packers and shoemakers and physicians. There was no such thing as just a burglar, Gerald said, and always when he said this he would bang a fist onto a table or into his palm. There were specific burglars and daredevil burglars and burglars who moved like turtles and burglars who darted in like spears. There were gentle burglars and semi-gentle burglars and of course there were the low-down sons of bitches who were never content unless they followed it up with a blackjack or switchblade or bullet. But the big thing to remember, Gerald would say, was this necessity of being a fine burglar, a clean and accurate operator, and honourable inside, damn it, an honourable burglar.

The big thing, Gerald would say, this thing of being honourable, was the only thing, and actually, if a human being didn't have it, there wasn't much point in going on living. As matters stood, life offered very little aside from an occasional plunge into luxurious sensation, which never lasted for long and even while it happened it was accompanied by the dismal knowledge that it would soon be over. In the winter Gerald had a mania for oyster stew, and always while he ate the stew he would complain the plate would soon be empty and his stomach would be too full for him to enjoy another plate. All these things like oyster stew and clean underwear and fresh cigarettes were temporary things, little passing touches of pleasure, limited things, unimportant things. What mattered, what mattered high up there by itself all alone, Gerald would say, was whether things were honourable.

Gerald would always come out strongly and challengingly with the contention that he himself was honourable and had always been honourable. Every promise he had ever made he had kept, even when it made him sick to do so, even when it placed him in actual jeopardy. There was a night when he had promised a girl he would marry her, and knew a moment later it would be a big mistake to marry her, to marry anyone. But he had promised. He couldn't break the promise. He married the girl and he stayed married to her until she died. Telling of it, he would yell and curse himself but he would always end up by describing her as a marvellous woman and it was a damn shame she had to go and die. And besides, Gerald would say, maybe the marriage had not been such a bad mistake, after all. In order for a man to be honourable within himself, it was necessary to carry some sort of a responsibility, a devotion. It was natural and correct that this devotion be aimed at a woman.

Looking back at the times long ago when Gerald had said all these things, Harbin heard them distinctly as though Gerald were talking aloud to him now. The sum of it was the centre of it, the core of it, this big thing, this being honourable. Gerald had taught him how to open the lock of a door, the lock of a vault, and how to analyze the combination of a safe, and how to get past certain types of burglar alarms, but the important thing Gerald had taught him was this thing of being honourable.

That was why, when he saw Gerald dead on the pavement, he had raced mechanically to get Gerald's daughter and why, all these years, he had looked after Gladden. That was the only thing for him to do, because it was the honourable thing.

Ahead of him, and rather near, the black bulk of the Million Dollar Pier took itself out upon the ocean. Just a little this side of the pier he saw the unlit electric sign of the hotel where Gladden was staying. It was a small hotel, hemmed in between boardwalk shops and apartments above the shops, but it had a certain independence about it, almost seemed to flaunt itself as one of the beachfront hotels, more dignified and elegant than the hotels of the boardwalk.

Walking in, he couldn't see anyone in the lobby. He hit the bell on the clerk's desk, hit it again and kept on hitting at it in intervals for more than a minute. Then the clerk came in from a side room and showed him a tired, yawning, aged face, some white hair far back on the head, a pair of tired, drooping shoulders.

Automatically the old man said, 'We got no rooms.' Then he began to wake up as he moved in behind the desk. 'Maybe,' he said, 'we got one empty.'

'I don't want a room.' Harbin was lost for a moment and then it came to him, the name she said she would use. 'I'm looking for Miss Green.'

'Nobody here by that name.' The old man started to move out from behind the desk, yawning again.

'Why don't you call Miss Green and then you can go back to sleep.'

'Buster,' the old man said, 'I'm going back to sleep right now and I ain't calling Miss Green because we ain't got no Miss Green.'

The old man was on his way to the side room when Harbin stepped into his path and showed him a couple of one-dollar bills.

'It's awfully important that I see Miss Green.'

The old man looked at the money. 'What was that name again?'

Harbin repeated it for him and spelled it for him.

'I think,' the old man said, 'maybe we got a Miss Irma Green.' Now he had the bills and was stuffing them into a vest pocket. 'But I'm ready to swear she checked out a couple days ago.'

'Let's make sure about that.'

The old man started back toward the desk and then stopped and circled his throat with his thin hand. 'She's a small, skinny girl? Blonde hair?'

Harbin nodded.

The old man made a face that was meant to be a smile, but it looked as though he was in pain. 'Miss Irma Green,' he said. 'Yes, a very nice little lady. Very nice indeed.'

'Call her for me, will you?'

The old man yawned again. He twisted his head and stared up at the wall-clock above the desk. 'You know,' he said, 'this ain't the best hour to go visiting people.'

'Call her.' Harbin indicated the phone. 'Just pick up the phone and call her room.'

'We got certain house rules.'

'I know you have. You got rules providing a guest with the right to know when she has a visitor.'

'Say, look, Buster,' the old man said. 'You standing there and arguing with me?'

Sliding his hand into his trouser pocket, Harbin took out more money, selected a five-dollar bill and showed it to the old man.

'All I want you to do,' he said, 'is put me on the phone as though it's an outside call.'

The old man thought it over for a moment. 'I guess there ain't no harm in that.'

Harbin gave him the money, frowned slightly while waiting for the switchboard to make contact. The old man nodded toward the phone, and Harbin took it and heard Gladden's voice.

He said, 'I'm calling from a few blocks away. I'll be there in five minutes. What's your room number?'

'Three one two. What's wrong? What's happened?'

'We'll talk about it when I see you.' He hung up and turned to the old man. 'I only want to see the man who's with her. You have my word there won't be any trouble. I won't even talk to him. I just want to see who he is.' He watched carefully to get the effect of his words on the old man. The effect was all right and it allowed him to add, 'He won't even get a look at me. I'll be in that side room and keep the door open. He won't even know I'm around.'

The old man was somewhat mixed up and worried. 'Well, all right,' he said, 'but we can't afford to have violence. A jealous husband comes to these places looking for his wife and he finds her with a boyfriend and right away we got a battle on our hands. Maybe you'll see him and you'll lose your temper.'

Harbin smiled. 'I'm not the jealous husband. I'm only a friend looking out for her welfare.'

He walked into the side room. It was black in there and he opened the door just wide enough to get a reasonable view of the lobby. He was halfway behind the door and from there he could see the old man fidgeting nervously near the desk. A minute passed, then another minute and Harbin put a cigarette in his mouth and began to chew on it. He watched the movement of the big hand on the wall-clock above the desk. The sound of a descending elevator came against his hearing and he saw the face of the old man turned toward him, the aged eyes very worried, the brow severely wrinkled. He heard the sound of the elevator as it came to a stop, and then the footsteps, and then he saw the double-breasted gabardine suit, the healthy crop of blond hair, the handsome features and aquamarine eyes of the young cop moving past his range of vision beyond the partly opened door.

CHAPTER XII

He waited there in the side room, unable to handle it. After the initial moments of amazement he knew it wouldn't do any good to think about it. It was something that went beyond thinking. He was scarcely conscious of the old man coming toward him, talking to him, telling him that he could come out now, the man had left the hotel and it was all right to come out now.

As he emerged from the side room into the lobby he heard the old man saying, 'Was it someone you know?'

Harbin shook his head.

'Then I guess everything's all right,' the old man said.

'Sure.' Harbin smiled, and stepped toward the elevator.

'Now hold on there.' The old man moved quickly between Harbin and the elevator.

'I promised there wouldn't be any trouble,' Harbin said. 'Besides, she's expecting me.'

The old man searched for some kind of a rebuttal, couldn't find any, made a gesture of surrender with his two hands and turned away from the elevator. Harbin entered the elevator, put a lit match to the cigarette in his mouth. He closed the elevator door and pushed the button.

As he entered Gladden's room, as he saw her stepping back and away from the door, the first thing he noticed was the white of her face. It was paper white and her yellow eyes were dull with some weird kind of fatigue. He wasn't smiling at her. He knew he ought to start this with a smile, but getting a smile started now would be like trying to walk on water.

'Start packing,' he said. 'Snappy.'

She didn't move. 'Tell me.'

'We're hot.' He knew there was no way of getting around it. Without looking at her, he said, 'Dohmer's dead.' He told her of what had happened on the road. He told her to hurry and start packing.

But she didn't move. She stood there gazing past him, at the door. He began taking her clothes from the narrow closet and throwing them on the bed. Then he had dresser drawers open and he was rapidly filling her suitcase.

He heard her saying, 'I can't go with you.'

That took him away from the suitcase. 'What's the rub?'

'I've met someone.'

'Oh.' He came back to the suitcase but didn't continue to fill it. She had her back to him and he was curious to see the condition of her eyes. He took a step toward her, then decided to stay where he was, to let her build it in her own way.

A long string of silent moments ended as she said, 'I want to get out, Nat. From now on I want to be out of it. I always wanted to be out of it but you kept me in.'

'How do you figure that?' he asked. 'I never told you to stay in against your will.'

'My will was to stay,' she said. 'Because of you.' Now she turned and faced him. 'I wanted to be near you. I wanted you and I wanted you to want me. But you didn't want me, you never wanted me, you never will. I've had a lousy time, I've gone through nights when I've torn pillows apart with my teeth, so hungry for you I wanted to smash down the wall and break into your room. You knew it, Nat. Don't tell me you didn't know it.'

He put his hands behind his back and cracked his knuckles.

Gladden said, 'All right, so I've never been much with brains. But it didn't need a lot of thinking. The point was, I went through something we all go through. I grew up. You didn't see it taking place but it was taking place all the time. I was growing up, from a little girl to a woman, and I wanted to be your woman. But what the hell could I do? I couldn't bang you over the head.'

'Maybe you should have tried that.' He sat down on the edge of the bed. 'This comes at a wonderful time.'

She moved toward him, reached out to touch him, then pulled her hand back. 'You've always been so good to me, you've taken care of me, you've been everything to me but what I was hoping you'd be. That isn't your fault. It isn't mine, either. It's just a miserable state of affairs.'

He smiled dimly. 'Miserable is one way of putting it.'

She detected the odd currents underneath his tone. She said, 'I hope you won't hold this against me.'

He looked up at her. 'What's his name?'

'Finley. Charles Finley.'

'What does he do? Tell me about him.'

'He sells automobiles. Salesman on a used car lot in Philly. I met him the second day I was here. On the boardwalk. We just got to talking and it happened sort of fast. I guess I was ripe for it, ready for it, he got me at just the right time, that night I went back to Philly and they told me you walked out and I came back here and called him up.'

'You really go for him?'

'He has a lot of charm.'

'I didn't ask you that.'

'All right,' she said, 'I think I go for him.'

Harbin stood up. 'When did you last see him?'

'He was here tonight. He was here when I got your call. When you said you were coming I told him to leave and I'd see him for lunch.' She took a deep breath. 'Don't ask me to break the date. I really want to see him, I want to keep on seeing him. I don't want to let him go.' She took hold of Harbin's arms. 'I won't let him go and you can't make me let him go.'

'Don't get wild,' he spoke gently.

'He's overboard for me,' she said, 'and if I told you I wasn't glad about that I'd be a no-good liar. I want to have some kind of a life for myself and you've got no right to keep me from having it.'

'Quit ripping my sleeves.' He frowned at her.

She was breathing very hard. Her fingernails cut through the fabric of his jacket. He twisted, got a grip on her wrists, forced her away. Going away, she staggered, bumped against a wall, stayed flattened against the wall, staring at him and taking deep, gasping breaths.

Harbin shook his head slowly. He gazed at the floor. 'It's a pity. It's a damned pity. It's a damned pity.'

'Not for me.'

He looked at her. 'Especially for you.' Then he waved her to quiet as she opened her mouth, and he said, 'Listen, Gladden, just listen to me and try to take it relaxed. You've been sucked in. This man is manipulating.'

'Don't.'

'This man, I tell you, is working on a job.'

'Don't. Please don't.'

'This man Finley is a cop—'

'Nat, Nat,' she cut in pleadingly. 'I told you I'm not a little girl anymore. I've grown up, I know the alphabet. Quit selling me short, will you?'

He was suddenly hit by too much weariness and he threw himself on his back on the bed, his arms flopping down, spread wide against the bedcover. 'If you'll try to listen,' he said, his eyes half-closed, 'I'll try to tell you. This Finley is one of the cops I talked to on the night we made the haul. A few minutes ago I was in a side room off the lobby as he came from the elevator and walked out. I recognized him.'

'Why are you doing this?' she cried. 'What are you trying to arrange?'

'I'm not doing the arranging. Finley's taking care of that.' Something like a sigh came from his lips. 'The cop angle doesn't mean anything. He holds on to that only for convenience. And from his position, you don't mean anything, either. He doesn't want you. He wants the emeralds.'

He saw her looking at him in a way she had never before looked at him. He heard her saying, 'Why do you lie to me?'

'Have I ever lied to you?'

'No,' she said. 'So why do you lie to me now?'

'I'm not lying. If you want all of it, I'll give you all of it.'

She nodded slowly, and he started to tell her. It was easy to start, but when he came to the Della proposition, he had trouble handling it, making it clear, moving ahead with it. She stood there and watched him as he struggled with it, as he managed to take himself back to the house on the hill and then the manoeuvring in Lancaster and the transit from the black woods to the road to the train to Philadelphia to the Black Horse Pike and to here and now.

He said, 'I can see Finley planning the thing, making sure there's no hitch. The day I took you to the train, he followed us. I can see him following us. He already had checked the Spot, and Della was watching the Spot. So there at the station when you got on the train, he got on, too. When you arrived here in Atlantic City, he was right behind you, watching you as you checked in at the hotel, then beginning to work on you here in Atlantic City while Della was working on me back there.'

She moved toward the bed, sat down on the edge of it. Her breathing had quieted somewhat. She said, 'Some people do things in a roundabout way.'

'Finley's way is not roundabout. It's quality from the word go. He has his eye on a hundred thousand dollars worth of emeralds. That's all. But that's plenty. He built this thing so it would work slowly, going upstairs a step at a time, first establishing the contact, bringing your guard down while Della brought mine down, figuring on a week or two weeks or three or maybe a couple of months. And even if it took six months and maybe even more than that, it was still a matter of a hundred thousand dollars and it would be worth all the trouble and all the waiting.'

She stared at the bedboard behind Harbin's head. 'Emeralds,' she said. 'Chunks of green glass.'

Harbin sat up just a little. 'Forget the emeralds,' he said. 'The major item is three dead policemen. That's something new with us.' He sat up completely, swung his legs over the side of the bed. 'It's why you've got to go with me. Stay with me. You're implicated, Gladden. I wish you weren't but you are. You and Baylock and myself. The three of us, we're in a situation where we've got to run. We've got to keep on running.'

'Are we that hot?'

'I don't know exactly how hot we are. I do know we can't stay around just in order to find out. If we move now, we'll be able to keep on moving.'

Gladden was quiet for a little while. Then she said, 'I thought I was out of it. The feeling I had was wonderful, like getting rid of a terrible throbbing headache that I'd had all my life. Now I'm back in again. I have the headache again.' She stood up, walked around the bed to the door, faced the door as though it was an iron wall. She turned again, coming toward him. 'You've pulled me back into it.'

'Circumstances.'

'Not circumstances.' There was a lack of reasoning in her eyes and in her voice. 'No, not circumstances. You. You, Nat. Keeping me in this time just like you've always kept me in. I tell you I don't want to be in.' Her entire body quivered. 'I don't want it, I don't want it, I never wanted it, I want to be out of it.' She came close to him. 'Out of it, out of it.'

'If you'll think it over,' he said, 'you'll see the point.'

Gladden said, 'There's only one reason you keep me around your neck. It's safer that way.'

He couldn't speak. The thing that crushed down on him was the sum weight of all the years, and her voice was a lance cutting through it, breaking it all up and showing him it added up to nothing but a horrible joke he had played on himself.

But he knew something more was coming, and he waited for it like a man tied to railroad tracks waiting for the impact. He looked at her and saw the whiteness of her face, the strange blaze in the yellow of her eyes.

And then it came. 'You bastard,' she said. 'You made me think you were looking out for me. You were looking out for yourself. You dirty tricky bastard, I hate your guts—'

He moved his head, but her arm was quicker, her extended fingers jabbed at his face, her fingernails ripping and he felt the slash, the icy burn. He saw her stepping back and away, her face twisted, her teeth showing.

'Here's your chance,' she said. 'Why don't you make it a real guarantee? Do what you've wanted to do all along. Get rid of me once and for all. Make sure I'll never talk and you'll always be safe.' She pointed at her throat. 'Look how skinny, how easy it would be. Take you no time at all.'

The door seemed to be moving toward him. As he opened it, with Gladden behind him, he waited and didn't know what he was waiting for. The room became quiet like a chamber with nobody in it. He opened the door wider, walked out, closed the door slowly as though Gladden was asleep in there and he didn't want to wake her up. He walked down the hall toward the elevator.

CHAPTER XIII

Baylock seemed dead except for his breathing, a sick troubled grinding breathing, the chest going up and down in a spasmodic way. Very little air was coming into the room and Harbin saw that he could open the window wider if he wanted to but he didn't have the inclination or the strength. He lowered himself onto the sagging bed beside Baylock and just before closing his eyes he told himself at least he ought to take off his shoes. But already he was going into sleep and his last conscious thought was that he had forgotten to put out the light and the light would have to stay on.

Almost eleven hours later Baylock woke him up. He asked Baylock what time it was and Baylock said three-fifteen. He rubbed his eyes and saw a thin slice of sunlight coming through the window after edging itself around the wall of the neighbouring building.

'I knew she wouldn't be there,' Baylock said.

'She was there.'

'Why didn't you bring her here?'

'She didn't want to come.'

'What's that again?'

Harbin was off the bed, moving toward a chipped washbowl. He put some cold water in his mouth, swished it around in there, put more in and swallowed it, put some on his face and turned and looked at Baylock.

'You'll like this,' he said. 'This is what you've been wanting.'

'Maybe you better wake up more,' Baylock was taking his turn at the washbowl. 'You're still from fog.'

'I'm wide awake,' Harbin studied Baylock at the washbowl. 'You wanted her out of it. All right, now she's out of it.'

Baylock frowned. 'How come?'

'That's the way she wants it.'

'You told her what happened?'

'I told her everything.'

'You told her everything,' Baylock said, 'and she wants to be out of it. Now, that's good. That's really pretty good. She finds out we got ourselves in a serious mess and we're wanted and she comes out with this interesting statement that she ain't with us any more.'

Harbin lit a cigarette. 'I can use some coffee.'

'Just like that,' Baylock said, 'she's out of it.'

'Let's get some coffee.'

Baylock didn't move. 'I'm too worked up to drink coffee. I'm too worried.'

'You don't know what worry is,' Harbin forced a smile. 'Here's real worry for you. Our friend made contact with her.'

'Our friend?' Baylock was far away from it.

'The cop.'

Baylock remained far away, unable to get himself to move any nearer.

Harbin said, 'His name is Finley. Charley Finley. He traced her down here and it seems he's that sun and salt air you were talking about.'

Reacting like an animal, Baylock made a move toward the door, changed his mind, started toward the suitcases, changed his mind about that, began to move here and there, darting little motions that got him back to where he had started. He whined, 'I told you, I told you, don't tell me I didn't tell you.'

'All right,' Harbin said. 'You told me. You were correct and I was wrong. Does that clear it up or do you want me to start chopping off my fingers?'

'We're hemmed in. Now we can't budge.'

'Why not? Finley doesn't know where we are.'

'You sure of that?' Baylock said. 'Look at the way he moves around. This is a trace artist. It's a very special gift. One in a million has it. Like a mind reader, a dealer in some kind of magic, and don't laugh, I tell you don't laugh.' He saw that Harbin was not laughing and he went on, 'For all we know he may have us spotted right now.'

'I wouldn't say that's impossible.'

'What do we do about it?' Baylock asked.

Harbin shrugged. He looked at the door. Then he looked at the window. Baylock followed his eyes. And then they looked at each other.

'The only way to know,' Harbin said, 'is to find out.' He frowned just a little, thinking it over. 'Finley could have followed me from her hotel last night. Followed me here. I doubt it and if I didn't know what he's done already

I'd bet a grand against a nickel it couldn't be possible.' He rubbed fingers across his chin. 'All I know for sure is I need some coffee. While I'm out I'll look around. You wait here.'

'How long?'

'Half hour.'

'Suppose it's longer.'

'It won't be.'

'But suppose it is?'

'In that case,' Harbin said, 'you'd better skip and skip fast.'

'With the emeralds?'

'Listen,' Harbin said. 'If it was you going out and me waiting here, and you said you'd be back in thirty minutes and you didn't come back in thirty minutes, I'd go for that window, and I wouldn't take the emeralds. And when I'd hit the street I'd start moving in a hurry.'

Baylock shook his head very slowly. 'I wouldn't leave the emeralds here. You know I wouldn't leave them here.'

Harbin shrugged.

Baylock said, 'If you're not back in thirty minutes, I'll start aiming toward my sister's place in Kansas City. You know the address and you know if I say I'm going there, I'm going there. And if you can manage to get there, you'll find me there with the emeralds.' He tightened his lips. 'Unless I'm grabbed before I can get there. Or dead.'

Harbin said, 'Should I bring you some coffee? Something to eat?'

'Just bring yourself back.'

Harbin started toward the door. Baylock moved quickly, with a kind of frenzy, went sliding in to place himself against the door, to face Harbin and show him a pair of disturbed eyes.

Baylock said, 'I want to get it straight about Gladden. What do we do with her?'

'Nothing.'

'What if she rats.'

'Why would she do that?' Harbin asked.

'She's out of it, that's why. When they're out of it they're in a position to rat. I'm worried, I tell you, and I think we ought to do something about Gladden.'

'Do this for me,' Harbin said. 'Don't mention her name.' He opened his mouth wide and something like a sob came out, and he turned his head quickly to hide his face from Baylock, and he took his fist and slammed it hard into his opened palm. He threw one swift glance at Baylock and saw Baylock looking at him with pity. It went into him like the orange end of a poker. He pulled the door toward him, went through and heard the door crash shut. He started fast down the narrow hall, came to the stairs and told himself to stop the rush. There was no need to rush. He was going out to take a look around and drink some coffee.

Downstairs, he could feel midday heat pouring in on him. It was like syrup. He felt his face get sticky and just a bit itchy. On the street moving slowly down Tennessee Avenue he saw the striped pole of a barber shop and decided on a shave.

The shave did something for him and he felt more alive as he came off Tennessee and hit Atlantic Avenue. But the sticky heat was really serious in Atlantic and the tingling effects of the shave were fading away while he looked around for a restaurant. Very few people were on the street. He saw some natives of the city walking across Atlantic in the direction of the beach. They seemed sullen, annoyed with their town for allowing itself to be messed up with this wet heat and angry at their ocean for not doing something about it. They wore beach robes and sandals and there was a sacrificial air about them as they headed toward the beach, as though this was something unfit for natives of Atlantic City at this time of year. It was all right for the vacationers because anything was all right for the vacationers, but natives of this town didn't deserve this weather, and it was an outrage.

He glanced at his wristwatch. Eight minutes. He had been out for eight minutes, and twenty-two minutes remained. A restaurant sign displayed itself on the other side of the street. He crossed and entered, sat down at a sloppy counter and told the waitress he wanted coffee. The waitress made a comment about how hot it was today for coffee, and maybe he would like it iced. He said he didn't want it iced. The waitress said it was good when it was iced. Harbin said he had never tried it iced and would appreciate their terminating the discussion; the waitress said the reason the world was like it was could be attributed to the fact that too many people were hard to get along with. She gave him a cup of black coffee and stood there watching him as he started on it. She was a short girl who looked Italian and restless, and below the short sleeves her fat arms were shiny with sweat. Harbin raised his eyes from the coffee and saw that she was watching him. He smiled at her. She took her eyes away from him and gazed through the opened doorway at the yellow, steaming street. She let out a long sigh and folded her arms and leaned back against the selling side of the counter.

Harbin glanced at his wristwatch and ordered another cup of coffee. She gave it to him and he lit a cigarette and began sipping the coffee, watching her as she stood there looking out toward the street. The sun came in and sent a yellow glaze all over her, so that it seemed as though she stood in the centre of a bowl filled with bright yellow syrup. She put out her tongue and licked some wetness away from her lip. Then a dark ribbon slanted across the yellow, so that she was in shadow and the shadow was caused by someone entering the restaurant. The Italian girl moved to greet the customer, and Harbin lowered his head toward the cup, started the coffee toward his mouth, felt the cup shake in his hands as the perfume hit him and he knew it was the perfume of Della.

CHAPTER XIV

Della sat down at the counter beside him. She wore an ivory-coloured blouse and skirt but even before he took note of her appearance he knew she would appear cool. Her tan hair gleamed in a quiet way, her face was quiet and cool, her voice cool as she told the waitress to fix her an orangeade.

Turning to look outside, Harbin saw the

green Pontiac parked on the other side of Atlantic. His fingers made a little drumbeat on the counter. 'You get around.'

'Only when it's necessary.'

He looked at her. 'What's necessary?'

'Being here,' she said. 'With you.'

'Unless I'm very much mistaken. I thought that was a dead issue.'

'You know it isn't dead.'

He worked on a little sigh and got it going. 'Tell me all about that.'

Della sat there looking at the orangeade. She said, 'I want you to do something for me. I want you to listen very carefully and try to believe what I'm saying. There's a chance you know already, but if you don't know, you'll hear it now. If you refuse to believe it, I can't do anything about that. It happens there are quite a few things I can't do anything about. Like turning night into day. Like stopping the rain when it's raining.' She turned fully to him.

She said, 'The night I met you there in that restaurant it was no accident. It was planned. A solid plan to have me work on you and get the emeralds. Of course you remember what happened the night you made the haul. You remember having a chat with two policemen outside the mansion? You remember that clearly?'

He nodded. He took a toothpick from a glass container, broke it in two and began to play with the pieces.

'One of them,' Della said, 'you saw was a rather young man. Early thirties. I want to tell you about that party. His name when he functions as a policeman is Charley Hacket. When he functions for the sake of Charley his last name is Finley.' She lifted the glass of orangeade, looked at it as though the colour pleased her, then put it down. 'This man Charley is out to get the emeralds. Most of the time he's a shakedown artist and he's usually satisfied with a cut. I know that because I know the way he operates. I've been working with him for a little more than a year. But this time he sees big loot and he wants all of it.'

Harbin took his eyes away from the toothpick production and he looked at her. He saw Della and nothing more than Della. Not the menace. Not the enemy in the woods. Only Della.

'This Charley Hacket,' she said, 'is very much from brains and when I first met him I could see that right away. And then of course I could see the looks he had and the charm and there was something else I thought he had and even when I found out he didn't have it I went on trying to believe it was there. When he asked me to work these jobs with him I did it only because it meant being with him. I certainly didn't need the money. And for sure I'm not the kind of mental case that does it for excitement. I did it because it meant being with him, and I had drilled it into myself that I needed to be with him. The night I changed my mind about that was the night I came across you.'

Harbin took another toothpick from the container and broke it in half. He put one piece at right angles to the other and then he switched them around. Then he pushed the bits of wood aside. 'Why did you wait until now? Why didn't you tell me all this before?'

'I was afraid,' she said. 'I wanted it to be just you and me, no emeralds, no Charley, no deals and transactions, just you and me. I was trying to work it out in my mind, find a method to slide away from Charley, get that ended so it would be just you and me. In order to do that I needed time. I wanted to tell you, I was dying to tell you. But I was terribly afraid of losing you.'

'Not afraid of Hacket?'

'No.' Then she gave a little shrug. 'I know the way it is with Hacket. I know I mean more to him than the emeralds. I know I'm his major weakness and he wants me more than he wants life. So what? So if he discovered the way I feel about you he would probably kill me. Or both of us. But I've never really been afraid of that. I've only been afraid of losing you. Last night in the woods when you walked away I had the notion of killing myself; the idea actually seemed attractive.'

She picked up the glass of orangeade and took some. She savoured it, took some more. 'I did a lot of thinking about it, knowing definitely that life is worthwhile only when you have a chance of getting what you want. I told myself if I couldn't have you it wouldn't pay to continue. All night long I thought about it and early this morning I was still thinking about it, ripping myself apart thinking about it when the phone rang and it was Hacket calling long distance from here, telling me you were here, wanting to know what went wrong. I told him I didn't know, I said you had just walked out on me without giving a reason. Hacket told me not to worry about that. He said it would work out much better this way—' She frowned just a little. 'I don't see any reaction. I thought you'd react when I said that Hacket was here in town.'

He smiled at her. 'Most of what you're telling me, I already know. I know he came here to work on Gladden.'

She sat there and stared at him. 'How did you find out? What put you on the track?'

'You did. I'll tell you all about it when we're old and grey. Maybe sooner.' He played with the toothpicks again. 'What did Hacket say on the phone?'

'He kept patting himself on the back, telling me how clever he was, the way he handled it when you came to her room at the hotel, how he waited in a doorway or someplace until you walked out on the boardwalk, how he followed you to that little dump off Tennessee Avenue.'

Harbin looked at Della, then at the toothpicks, then at Della again.

Della said, 'I told him I was coming to Atlantic City. He said no, he could handle it alone. I told him he shouldn't get too hasty and I was coming here and we wouldn't discuss it further. He said he'd be sitting in his car, parked on Tennessee Avenue, keeping an eye on your hotel. I met him there and said I'd take over. I said he looked beat and it would be a good idea if he went back to his room and got some sleep. We fought about that for a while but finally he gave in. I backed my car up on Tennessee Avenue, waited there, and then I saw you coming out from the side street. Then and there I would have called to you but I saw you going into a barber shop and I knew we couldn't talk in a barber shop. So I waited.

And when you came out, I followed you. And here I am now, I'm here with you, and I want to stay with you, go with you—'

'Where?'

'Our place.'

His head went down, then it came up very slowly, then down again. And he was nodding. And then he trembled suddenly, as though trying to pull himself out of a trance. He tasted metal in his mouth, trembled again, went very deep into himself and said, 'It's got to be figured out.'

'Let's figure it.'

'There's Hacket.'

'We'll get rid of him.'

Harbin leaned his elbow on the counter. 'I guess there's no other way of getting around it.'

'No other way,' she said. 'It will have to be done.' She took more orangeade. 'Anything else?'

He looked at her. He didn't say anything.

She said, 'You're thinking of Gladden.'

He took his eyes away from her. He didn't say anything.

She said, 'Do something for me. Stop thinking of Gladden.'

It was difficult, but he managed to do that for her. He worked at it, pushed with his mind as though he was heaving against a wall with his shoulder. He felt the resistance, and then strangely and suddenly it melted away but there was something else, and he said, 'There's something else.'

'All right, we'll face it. What is it?'

'It's a situation. Maybe you saw the papers today. Maybe you didn't.' He gave way to a sigh. 'Last night there was some heavy trouble on the Black Horse Pike.'

He told her of the three policemen who had died from bullets on the Pike, and of how Dohmer had died, and of what was now happening to Baylock, the fear and the worry, the lack of control, Baylock jittery, Baylock more or less immobilized. And he said, 'I can't walk out on Baylock without first telling him about it.'

'What good will it do?'

'He needs assurance. He needs instructions. I can't leave him with the feeling he's being let down. I've got to go back to the room and have a talk with him.'

'He'll argue with you.'

'I'll meet all his arguments.'

'He'll get excited. Maybe you'll have trouble.'

'There won't be any trouble.'

'He'll think you're trying to put something over.'

'He won't have any reason to think that,' Harbin said. 'I'm letting him have all the emeralds. Then I'm saying goodbye to him. Then I'm coming back here. To you. We'll get in your car and we'll start driving. We'll go to the place on the hill and we'll stay there together. I know for sure now that's the only way it can be. Nothing can break this up between you and me. Nothing. It was bound to be this way. We have something here that neither of us can get away from. When I left you there in the woods last night, you were someone else and I was someone else. But last night was a long time ago.'

He put some silver on the table and stood up. He smiled at her and he saw her smiling back at him and he didn't want to leave, even though it was firm in his mind that he would be returning within minutes. Then Della nodded toward the door, her eyes telling him to go and come back quickly. He left the restaurant and crossed Atlantic Avenue and walked fast toward Tennessee. He came onto Tennessee and walked faster as he approached the narrow side street. Entering the hotel, he felt light, his head was clear.

In the upstairs hall the heat was dark and thick and carried the decay of the people who lived in these rooms. Harbin came to the door and opened it and the first thing he saw was two suitcases wide open, their contents flung around. The third suitcase, the one containing the emeralds, was closed. The next thing he noticed was Baylock. On the floor, knees bent, Baylock had one arm across his eyes and the other arm rigid behind him. Baylock's eyes were very wide and the pupils were trying to climb into his forehead. Blood from his hammered head was bright and flowing and spilling down from the split skull in a wide stream that stayed wide as it reached the shoulder, then became a glistening red ribbon headed toward the elbow. Baylock was almost dead and while Harbin stood there and looked at him he tried to open his mouth to say something. This was as much as Baylock could do, and in the middle of trying to open his mouth, he pulled back his head and died.

CHAPTER XV

Harbin allowed his head to turn slowly and he looked at the unopened suitcase. It told him what he needed to know, but it was a matter of reaching a conclusion and not being able to do anything about it. He wouldn't have time to make the door, and the window was foolish. The closet door, partly open, now opened wider, and Charley Hacket came out of the closet with a revolver. The butt that had smashed Baylock's head was red with Baylock's blood.

'For Christ's sake,' Harbin said, 'don't use that thing, keep your head. Whatever you do, keep your head.'

'Shut up.' Hacket's voice was smooth pebbles on velvet. 'Get on the bed, face down.'

Harbin put himself on the bed and let his face go into the pillow. He saw himself receiving it as Baylock had received it. His lips moved against the pillow. 'This won't gain you anything.'

'Quit bargaining,' Hacket said, 'unless you have something to sell.'

Harbin had his brain focused on the unopened suitcase, the suitcase Hacket had been about to open when footsteps coming down the hall had told Hacket to slide into the closet. He wondered what Hacket was doing now. He wondered whether Hacket was looking at the suitcase.

'Where are the emeralds?'

There was a sudden hysteria in Hacket's tone and Harbin grabbed at it as though it were a rope dangling toward him with quicksand the only other thing around.

Harbin said, 'It's got to be business.'

'You're in no position to talk business.'

'You want the emeralds?'

'Now.'

'That's an order I can't fill,' Harbin said. 'I can't manufacture emeralds for you. All I can do is take you to where you'll find the haul.'

There was a quiet. Then Hacket told him to turn around.

Harbin turned, started to sit up and Hacket said, 'What I don't like about you is you're too scared.'

'Sure.' Harbin inclined his head toward the gun. 'What have I got to be scared about?' He indicated the gun. 'Just be sensible, Charley. That's all I ask. Be sensible.'

'All right, I'll be sensible. I'll ask you a sensible question. Where are the emeralds?'

'If I tell you,' Harbin said, 'you'll kill me anyway. And even then you have no guarantee I was telling the truth.'

'We can't get around that.'

'Be smart, Charley. I don't have to give you ideas. You know how to frame ideas.'

'What are you pitching?'

'No pitch, Charley. Just trying to stack things up and get a total. There's you, there's me, there's the emeralds. And—'

'And that's all.'

'That isn't all.' Harbin said it slowly and with great emphasis. He waited.

He saw the hysteria in Charley Hacket's eyes and in the little jerky movement of the underlip. He knew he had to depend on the hysteria but he couldn't depend on it too long, because it was the hysteria that had caused Hacket to go in for killing. It was hysterical impatience that had brought Hacket up to this room, pure compulsive ignition working Hacket's arm to bring the gun butt crashing into Baylock's skull. Harbin told himself he was dealing with a certain kind of twisted personality and at any moment the gun might go off.

He heard Hacket saying, 'What else is there?'

'The girl.'

'The girl,' Hacket said, 'is nowhere. Is nothing. You can't tell me nothing about the girl.' Then the lips worked up a little at the corners, the teeth showed and it was almost a smile. 'You've known her for years and I've only known her for days. But I think I know her better than you.'

'You don't even know her right name.' Harbin sat up straighter. 'Her name isn't Irma Green. Her name is Gladden. Now if you want it, I'll let you have it.' Without waiting, he went on, 'You were sucked in, Charley. She lured you in. You started the game but after that it was strictly her play. You were handed a fast hustle and don't be too surprised now when I tell you she has you down pat, you're in the palm of her hand, she can do whatever she wants with you.'

The corners of Hacket's lips came down. 'She knows from zero.'

'From plenty.'

'Like what?'

'Your identity.'

'My face?' Hacket chuckled for a moment. 'What's a face?'

'I don't mean your face, Charley, I mean your name. Not the name you gave her, not Charley Finley. I mean the other name, the real name, the name you didn't want her to know. But she found out.'

Hacket stared. 'You're a liar.'

'Sometimes,' Harbin admitted. 'But not at this point. I tell you Gladden found out. Don't ask me how. I've never been able to figure the way she operates. All I know is, she thinks a hundred moves ahead of anyone she's dealing with. That goes for me as well as you.'

Hacket threw a hand toward the back of his head and rubbed his hair up and down. 'What did she tell you my name was?'

'Hacket.'

Hacket said quickly and loudly, 'How did she find out? Tell me how she found out.'

'I asked her that and she told me to go get her a drink of water. So I went and got her a drink of water. You see, Charley, I work for her. You see how it is? She's the head figure. She gives the orders. She's in charge of everything. You see what I'm getting at?'

'Say it, God damn you. Go on and say it.'

'Gladden has the emeralds.'

Behind the gun the face became hard wax, becoming white and whiter as the lips stiffened. The aquamarine eyes looked down at the gun and then looked at Harbin. The eyes frightened Harbin and he wondered how much longer he would be alive in this room. He knew the chances were that in less than a minute from now he wouldn't be alive. He realized he had made a good try and he had pushed it across as well as it could be gotten across. But the one thing he couldn't handle was the fact that Hacket was very hysterical and in the mood to kill. He wondered if there was anything he could say.

He said, 'Neither of us want to die.'

'I'm holding the gun.'

'The gun,' Harbin said, 'is a minor item. I'm not talking about the gun. I'm talking about the rap.' He indicated Baylock on the floor. 'There's something.' He said it as though it was comparatively important, and then he put the big worry out in from where they could both look at it. 'Maybe you saw the papers this morning.'

'No.'

'Last night. On the Black Horse Pike. All they did was stop us for speeding. Three of them in a patrol car. One of them saw one of us with a gun. That started it. The business ended with all of them dead and one of us dead.' Again he indicated the body on the floor. 'Now we have that. And don't you think that's enough grief for this party?'

'I want the emeralds.'

'As hot as they are?'

'I want them.'

'As far as I'm concerned, you can have them.'

'I don't believe you.' Hacket moved in a little to aim the revolver at Harbin's stomach. 'You still want them, don't you? Don't you?' The teeth showed. 'Don't you?'

'No,' Harbin said, wanting to say it again, wanting to plead, knowing it wouldn't do any good to plead. Just then he heard the sound in the hall outside near the door. He saw Hacket's head turning and knew Hacket was hearing it.

The sound was directly outside the door and the next thing was knuckles against the door. Then they both heard her voice. Hacket opened the door, keeping the gun on Harbin.

As Della walked in, her eyes were pulled to the red on the floor and Baylock's dead face resting against the shiny red. She turned away quickly from that. She waited until Hacket had closed the door and then she stared at him. Her voice was low and quivered just a little. 'What are you, a lunatic?'

Hacket stood looking at the door. 'I couldn't help it.'

'That means you're a lunatic.' Della glanced briefly at Harbin. Her head turned slowly, her eyes came back to Hacket. 'I told you to wait in your room.'

Hacket blinked a few times. 'I've had too much waiting. I got fed up with waiting.'

'I'm getting fed up with you.' Della pointed to the dead body on the floor. 'Look at that. Just look at it.'

'Quit giving me hell.' Hacket blinked a few more times. 'I'm having enough hell.' Suddenly he frowned at her. 'What made you come here?'

'I called your room.' The quivering had gone out of her voice. 'There was no answer.' Her eyes were drawn back to Baylock on the floor. She moved strangely toward the body and all at once she whirled and came toward Hacket and cried, 'What in God's name is the matter with you?'

'I want to get this thing ended.'

'You worried?'

'Sure I'm worried.'

'Quit worrying.' Hacket suddenly smiled widely. He seemed extremely pleased about something. 'I'm glad you're here. It's a good thing you came. You couldn't have come at a better time. That's one of the nicest things about you, Della. You always know just when to arrive.' As he finished it, he sent the smile toward Harbin. 'Thank the lady,' he told

Harbin. 'If she hadn't walked in, you'd be dead now.'

'I know that.' Harbin nodded seriously. He looked at Della, his face expressionless. 'Thanks, lady.'

Hacket continued to smile. He gestured with the gun. 'Say it again.'

'Thanks, lady. Thanks very much.'

'Now say it once more—' Hacket began to laugh. He let his head go far back and his body vibrated with the laughing. It was sick laughing and it was getting louder. Della waited until the laughing filled the room and then she stepped in close to Hacket and sent the back of her hand across his face. He went on laughing and Della hit him again. While she hit him he had his eyes wide open and aiming along with the gun at Harbin.

Della hit Hacket hard across the face and gradually the laughing stopped. Hacket blinked a great many times. He began to shake his head slowly as though trying to figure himself out and couldn't do so. After some moments he gazed pleadingly at Della and stood there and waited for her to say something. When she didn't respond to this, Hacket pulled himself away from the depth of himself, came up to the surface of himself, showed it in the way he pushed his chest out, lifted his chin, set his feet solidly against the floor. A brightness came into the aquamarine eyes and it was surface brightness. Harbin realized Hacket was trying to re-establish himself with himself and with Della. It seemed that Hacket believed fully in his ability to do this.

Hacket's tone was in harmony with the way he stood there. 'The girl's name is Gladden. Now, I pay her a visit and when I walk in I call her Irma, Irma Green. And when I walk out I have the emeralds.' He glanced at Della. 'When I come back here I have the emeralds and you'll be waiting here for me.' He looked at Harbin. 'You'll be here, too, and once I have the emeralds I'll be in a happy frame of mind, maybe I'll let you walk out of here alive. Remember, I say maybe, I don't guarantee anything.'

Harbin was thinking of Gladden. He tried hard not to believe that Hacket was going out to kill Gladden. He heard Hacket talking to Della but the words didn't mean anything, the words were vague symbols blanketed by the realization that he was saving his own life at the expense of Gladden's life. In order to keep from dying, he had decided to use something, and he had used Gladden. He saw Gladden dying. He saw Gladden dead. He closed his eyes and saw it and felt it. Then he opened his eyes and looked at Della. He told himself it would be all right. Soon he would be here alone in the room with Della and together they would know how to work it out, they would scheme a way to get to Gladden before Hacket got to her. They would work it out. He told himself he was sure it would all be all right.

His head came up and he saw Della. She looked deeply thoughtful. Then a different look came onto her face as Hacket offered her the gun. Hacket was moving toward the door. Della stood still with the gun in her hand, showing it to Harbin, showing him the look on her face that was a puzzling kind of look, the kind of look he had never seen on her face before. Now Hacket was at the door. The strange look stayed on Della's face. It began to bother Harbin. He heard Hacket opening the door.

He heard Hacket saying, 'This won't take long. Just hold him here and entertain him until I get back.'

The door opened and Hacket walked out.

CHAPTER XVI

Harbin looked at the closed door and heard the footsteps going away down the hall, then going down the stairs and fading. He felt his head turning toward the gun in Della's hand.

It was time for her to lay the gun aside. The gun remained in her hand. The strange look remained on her face. His eyes asked her why she was pointing the gun at him and her eyes gave him no answers.

He said, 'We didn't arrange it this way. Why did you come here?'

'You heard what I told Charley. That's it. I had a feeling. I phoned his room and he wasn't there. I just had a feeling.'

'That isn't enough.' For a moment he forgot about the gun. His eyes went into her. 'How did you know it was this room?'

'Charley had given me the number.'

Harbin took his eyes from her and stared at the wall behind her head. 'I'm wondering how Charley knew the room number.'

'He got it when he followed you here last night. When he follows people he really follows them. He had his eyes on you from the time you walked up here.'

'Charley's brilliant.'

'You're brilliant too.' Her face did not change. 'What took place here? What did you sell him?'

'He came to get the emeralds and after he killed Baylock he opened two suitcases. He was about to open the third when I arrived. I had to talk him out of shooting me. He was very anxious to shoot me.'

Della looked at the unopened suitcase. 'They in there?'

Harbin nodded. He made a gesture to indicate that she should put the gun aside. The gun stayed on him.

His lips pressed hard against his teeth. 'What are you doing?'

'Keeping you here.'

'Like Charley ordered?'

'Charley had nothing to do with it.'

'Then why?' he asked. 'What do you want?'

'It's not what I want. It's what I don't want. I don't want you to go away.'

'I'm not going away. I only want to get to Gladden before Charley gets to her. He's out to kill her. You understand that, don't you? You know as well as I, we're up against a time element.'

Della spoke slowly. 'I'm giving Charley all the time he needs.'

'Della—'

'I want him to kill her.'

Harbin was up and away from the bed. He was moving toward the gun.

Della pushed the gun at him. 'Stand back. You try to take it from me and I'll pull the trigger. Then I'll pull it on myself.'

Harbin felt very weak. He leaned against the edge of the bed. 'You really want me that much?'

'There's nothing else I want.'

'Thanks.' He smiled weakly. 'Thanks for loving me so much. But I can't let Gladden die.'

'I can't let her live.'

'You're crazy jealous. If you saw me looking at the clouds, you'd be jealous of the clouds.'

Della said, 'I can't get rid of the clouds. I can certainly get rid of Gladden.' Her voice climbed a little. 'I won't let you hold on to Gladden.'

'Believe me, will you?' He could feel a fever in his brain. 'I swear to you, there's nothing there.'

'There's everything.' And all at once she was smiling sadly and her voice was very sad. 'You don't realize it, my sweet, but that's the way it is. Your entire life is Gladden. Last night in the woods you walked away from me, but you really didn't want to walk away. It was Gladden, pulling you, dragging you away.'

He lifted his hands, bent his fingers, pushed them hard into his shut eyes. 'I can't remember. I don't know what it was.'

'I tell you it was Gladden. I want to release you from that. I want to cure you of this sickness you have. This sickness from all the way back. Her father.'

He stared at Della and she nodded and said, 'Gerald, Gerald,' and he felt as though he was being strangled.

Della said, 'All you could do was tell me the story. You couldn't figure it. I had to do the figuring for myself.'

He reached out and gripped the wood post of the bed and tried to crush the wood.

He heard Della saying, 'You're controlled by a dead man.'

'No.'

'Gerald.'

'No.'

'Gerald,' she said. 'This man who picked you up and kept you alive when no one else gave a good God damn. You were a kid there, standing in the road. You were dizzy and starving, you were sick, and the cars went past, one after another. They didn't even look at you. But Gerald looked. Gerald picked you up. And that was it, that was your wonderful luck. It had to be Gerald who picked you up, Gerald who cared for you, fed you, put clothes on you, schooled you. Everything was Gerald. His ideas became your ideas. His life became your life. Now listen carefully while I tell you that when Gerald died his daughter became your daughter.'

The room closed in on Harbin. The walls slanted and moved down on him. He could feel the nearness of the moving walls.

He heard her saying, 'All these years you've been ruled by it. Every move you make, guided by Gerald. Always, every minute, asleep or awake, Gerald telling you what to do, how to do it—'

'Please, will you?' He shouted it. 'Shut up.'

'I want you to break loose. Be free of it once and for all.'

Harbin heard something that sounded like, 'Really, I can't do that. It wouldn't be honourable.' He wondered where the voice was coming from. He wondered whether it was coming from his own lips or whether it was some other voice that he could hear inside himself. He was looking at the door. He moved toward the door and the gun followed him. He knew it followed him and he knew it was a gun and what it could do. He went toward the door.

'I'll shoot you,' Della said. 'I'll shoot you dead.'

He was past the edge of the bed and he heard Gerald telling him to take the haul. He walked past Della and picked up the unopened suitcase and went on toward the door. He heard Gerald telling him to hurry. The door was in front of him as he sensed the pointed gun behind him. He heard a sob coming from behind him. The door was opening. He continued to move, feeling the heaviness of the suitcase. Then from behind him he heard the sob again, and then a sound like a thud, and he knew it was the gun hitting the floor. Now the door was closed behind him. He was in the hall. For another moment he could hear the sobbing in the room behind him but something caused him to stop hearing it and the only thing behind him was Gerald, urging him down the hall, urging him toward Gladden.

CHAPTER XVII

On the boardwalk, he approached the hotel, he saw the sun hitting the silvery rail that separated the raised boards from the beach. There were a lot of people on the beach and most of them wore bathing suits. The beach was white-yellow under the sun. He looked at the ocean and it was flat and passive, with the heavy heat coming down on it, giving it the look of hot green metal. The waves were small and seemed to lack enthusiasm as they came up against the beach. In the water the bathers moved slowly, without much enjoyment, getting wet but not cool. He knew the water was warm and sticky and probably very dirty from the storm of Saturday night. Even so, he told himself, he would like to be in there in the ocean with the bathers, and maybe he and Gladden would have themselves a swim before leaving Atlantic City. The thought was an extreme sort of optimism but he repeated the thought and kept repeating it as he moved toward the entrance of the hotel.

The old man was there behind the desk and

Harbin came up to him and smiled and said, 'When do you sleep?'

'Snatches.' The old man was doing something to his thumbnail with the point of a pen.

Harbin put down the suitcase. 'I'd like to see Miss Green.'

The old man pushed the pen-point against the cuticle. 'It's a scorcher. It's a real scorcher today.' He looked at Harbin. 'For this time of year it's what I call flukey weather. I never seen such rotten heat. This town ain't had a day like this in twenty years.'

'Miss Irma Green.'

'You look melted down,' the old man said. 'We got a bath-house here. Want to get into a suit?'

'I want to see Miss Green. Call her, will you please?'

'She's out.'

'Checked out?'

'No, just went out.'

'Alone?'

The old man showed a perfect set of teeth that spent part of each night in a glass of water. 'You make me out to be an information desk.' He worked the pen-point against the side of his thumbnail, looked up sufficiently to see the bill in Harbin's fingers. He took the bill from

Harbin, crumbled it in his fist, then let it slide into the breast pocket of his grimy shirt. 'She went out alone.'

'When?'

Turning his head slowly, his chin raised, the old man studied the wall-clock. It said four-thirty. 'Must have been a couple hours ago.'

'Has the man been here since then?'

'What man?'

'You know who I mean?'

'I don't know anything unless I'm told about it.' The old man glanced calmly toward the little bulge in the breast pocket of his shirt, then his eyes travelled to the wall across the lobby and stayed there.

'I mean the man who was here last night,' Harbin said. 'The good-looking man with the blond hair. The man I watched from the little room while he walked out.'

'Oh,' the old man said. 'That man.' He waited a few moments, then he was too old and too weary to be ambitious for more money. 'Yes, that man was here. Came in about twenty minutes ago. I told him she wasn't in and he hung around long enough to light a smoke. You smoke?'

Harbin gave the old man a cigarette, lit it for him. 'Mind if I wait here?'

'Make yourself comfortable.'

There was a sofa and a few chairs. He let the suitcase remain where it was and sat in the sofa and after some minutes he checked the suitcase with the old man and strolled out of the lobby, walked across the boardwalk to the rail and stood there looking at the entrance of the hotel. He went through a few cigarettes, discovered that he was ready to eat something. The hotel was flanked by souvenir stores and sandwich stands that opened on the boardwalk. He bit into a ham-and-cheese sandwich, downing it with coffee while his eyes focused on the entrance of the hotel. He had another sandwich, some more coffee and then he bought a couple of newspapers and walked into the hotel and took the sofa again.

Later, much later, it seemed to him that he had covered every word in both newspapers. He glanced at his wristwatch and it put the time at close to seven. The sun was still going strong outside, and he was relieved to see the sunlight. Bringing his eyes back to the lobby he saw the old man behind the desk, working on another fingernail.

He went back to the newspapers. It became seven-thirty. It became eight. Then eight-fifteen and eight-thirty. He was out of cigarettes and as he put the papers aside he sensed night coming in from the boardwalk. He looked toward the door and saw it was black out there.

Near the door there was a cigarette machine and he was taking the pack from the slot when someone came into the lobby and pulled his eyes up and he saw it was Gladden. He said her name and she turned and stared at him.

He moved toward her. She wore a hat that looked very new. It was a small hat, a pale and powdery orange, nothing on it but a long pin with a bright orange plastic head, like a big round glistening drop of juice.

Getting in close, Harbin kept his voice low. 'We skip. We got to do it now.'

He wasn't looking at her but he knew her eyes were on him. He heard her saying, 'I told you I was out of it.'

'Not yet.'

She bit hard into each word. 'I'm out of it.'

'Your friend Charley doesn't know that.' He took her arm.

She pushed him away. 'Go, will you? Just go. Get away from me.'

'Let's walk the boards.' He turned his head a little and saw curiosity on the face of the old man.

Gladden said, 'I want you to leave me alone. For the rest of my life I want to be left alone.'

'The rest of your life is a matter of minutes

if you don't let me help you.'

Now he was looking at her and he saw it coming onto her face. It began with the eyes, and after the eyes widened, the lips parted and she could just about get the words out. 'I won't be bothered by Charley. So he is what he is. So what? There's no reason why Charley should bother me. I'm not scared of Charley.'

'You're plenty scared,' he said. 'You're paralyzed. You're so stiff you haven't been able to budge. So much in a fog you didn't have the brains to pack up and leave town. All you could do was float along the boardwalk and buy yourself a hat.' He turned, moved across the lobby, handed the old man some change and came back with the suitcase. Gladden looked at the suitcase. Harbin smiled and nodded and then he was taking her out of the lobby, onto the boardwalk. It was still very hot out, but now the beginning of a breeze came in from the ocean. The boardwalk lights made a curving parade of yellow spheres against the black, curving out to meet the majestic brilliance of the big pier, the entertainment bazaar, the white blaze of it far up ahead, Steel Pier.

'My arm,' she said.

He realized he was pressing too hard. He let go. In front of him, a mile away, the lights of Steel Pier dazzled his eyes, and he blinked. He felt his walking motion on the boards, and Gladden walking beside him. He saw the other people on the boardwalk and it was a satisfying thing to see them there, all out there on the boardwalk to get the breeze.

Gladden moved a step out in front of him to gaze up at his face. 'Why did you come back?'

He was lighting a cigarette. He got it lit, took in the taste of it, a harsh taste now after all the previous cigarettes. But still it tasted good, and the wood of the boardwalk felt good under his feet. He puffed at the cigarette, and then, his voice coming easily, he told her why he had come back. He made it as technical as he could, getting in all the details without elaborating on them. When he was finished they had covered half the distance to Steel Pier. He smiled dimly, contentedly at all the lights and all the people between his eyes and the Pier, and he waited for Gladden's voice.

She wasn't saying anything. Her head was down and she was looking at the shiny wood of the boardwalk as it went flowing past her moving feet.

'Thanks,' she said. 'Thanks for coming back.'

Her voice was grey and dismal, the heaviness of it came against him. He frowned, 'What's wrong with you?'

'I have a feeling. Maybe it would have been better the other way.' Before he could reply, she murmured, 'Nat, I'm tired.'

There was a pavilion close by, and he took her to it. The pavilion was a little more than half filled, mostly middle-aged people who sat there with nothing on their faces. There were some children moving restlessly among the benches, and a man wearing a white marine cap was selling bricks of ice cream.

The bench Harbin selected was toward the middle of the pavilion where it went away from the boardwalk to hover over the beach. As he came against the bench he felt the secure comfort of it and he looked at Gladden and saw that she was leaning her head far back, her eyes closed, her mouth set in a tight line.

He said, 'That's a nice hat you bought.'

She didn't respond. Her face stayed the way it was.

'Really an elegant hat,' he said. 'You got good taste.'

Gladden opened her eyes and looked at him. 'I wish you hadn't come back.'

'Quit talking foolish.' His lips curved upward in a scolding smile. 'This isn't the time to talk foolish. What we do now is plan. We have the opening and what we do is use it.'

'For what good reason?'

'To stay alive.'

'I'm not too sure that I want to stay alive.'

Harbin sent his eyes toward the broadwalk in front of him, where the parade of people was a stream of mixed pastels. He shook his head slowly and sighed heavily.

'I can't help it,' Gladden said. 'That's the way I feel.' She put a hand to her eyes. 'I'm tired. I'm so tired of keeping it in, holding it back, the way I feel.' She began to breathe like a marathon runner finally giving up. 'I can't go on with it anymore. There's nothing to gain.'

'That's right.' He looked at her. 'Make it complicated. Make it miserable.'

'I've always made it miserable for you.' She made a move to take his arm, then pulled her hand away. 'All I've ever done was hold you back.'

'Let's do the smart thing. Let's let it ride.'

'Ride where?' she asked, then answered it. 'Nowhere.' Now she took his arm, but only to make him pay close attention. 'The way it lines up, it's no good. Last night,' and now there was a choking in her voice, 'I threw you out of my room. I called you names because I couldn't tell you what I really felt. I've never been able to tell you what I feel. Until now. Because now it's like when they say the time has come. Like in a story I read once where there's a walrus and he says the time has come.'

Her hold on his arm was very tight and he wondered for a moment if that was where the pain was. And then he knew it wasn't in his arm.

'So now,' she said, 'the time has come. I love you, Nat. I love you so much I want to die. I really want to die, and whether it comes from Charley or no matter how it comes, I don't care, I just want to die. You see,' and she turned her head away from him, not wanting him to see, 'it's no good when you're sad all the time.'

He tried to get rid of the big heavy thing in his throat. 'Don't say that.' He knew it only made things worse and wanted so much to make things better and didn't know how. 'I've given you one hell of a rotten trip.'

'Not your fault. Not the least bit your fault.' She took her hand away from her arm. 'I get the blame. I knew I wasn't needed, so what did I do? I hung around. Like a leech.' Her eyes, condemning herself, were dreary yellow. 'That's all I've ever been. A leech.' And then, the lips barely moving, 'The only time a leech comes in handy is when it dies.'

For an instant he wasn't able to move, to breathe, to think. It was the complete stillness that comes just before a cannonade. And as the thing hit the sky and split the black apart, he told himself it was love. He drilled it, with a hard and wild frantic drilling, telling himself it was love, drilling it into himself as his arms shot out to take Gladden, to pull her against himself and hold her there. With him.

'You won't get away,' he said. 'I'll never let you get away.'

Staggered, dazed, her eyes reaching toward Harbin's eyes, the softness of her voice covered the screaming inside. 'You do care?' And then, her voice still soft, 'You do care. You do, you do, I know you do.'

'I do.' Just then the knowledge came and he understood what it all was, and who had sent the cannonade, and who had done the drilling, who had moved his arms for him and kept his arms where they were now. He knew it with complete knowing. He knew it was Gerald and it was Gerald causing him to say it as he said, 'I love you, Gladden.'

CHAPTER XVIII

The breeze coming in from the ocean was swifter now, and the news of the breeze must have reached the streets, because more people were coming onto the boardwalk and arriving there with pleasure on their faces. Lit brightly with the faces and the lights, the white lights of the boardwalk lampposts and the coloured lights of the boardwalk shops and cafes and hotels, the boardwalk was a ribbon of movement and high glow, many colours and many sounds, sparkling there, its brightness slicing the black of sky and beach and ocean.

From the boards there was a steady flow of people coming into the pavilion and it became filled. The man selling ice cream was doing good business, and a competitor saw what was happening and moved mechanically toward the pavilion. The people sat there and bought ice cream and took in the breeze, feeling the cool of it, breathing in the salt of it, content to sit there and take it. There was very little talking in the pavilion. They were there to get the breeze.

Harbin wanted more talking, more sound. It was time, he knew, to shape a plan and he couldn't very well talk plans with Gladden against this quiet. He turned his head and looked toward the rear of the pavilion where it hung over the beach. There was one empty bench and it was on the last row, set close to the rail and somewhat isolated. The edge of it was near the stairs going down to the beach. He stood up with the suitcase and Gladden followed him to the rear of the pavilion and they took the bench. Ahead of them there was a slight scurry as some people raced toward the bench they had vacated. There was some pushing and shoving up there and the beginning of an argument. The voices climbed, an elderly woman called another woman a name and was called a name in return and that more or less settled it and the pavilion was quiet again.

'Let's figure it.' He lit a cigarette. Gladden leaned against his shoulder and the pale gold under his eyes was her hair flowing across his chest, gliding in the breeze.

'Money,' Gladden said. 'All my cash is in the room. We'll have to go back.'

'No.' His thoughts were moving out across a mixture of chequerboard and blueprint. 'I'm carrying enough. Almost seven grand.'

'Big bills?'

'Mostly.'

'That's a problem.'

'Not for a while. There's enough tens and fives to keep us moving.' He took a long pull at the cigarette. 'What bothers me is transportation.'

He looked up at the jet sky. It was sprinkled heavily with stars and there was a full moon. Between the stars and the moon he traced a pattern of travel, sending a map up there and seeing Gladden and himself moving across the map, going somewhere. He wondered where. He wondered how long it would take to get there, and whether they would ever get there. The map in the sky became a dismal map and he told himself to quit looking at it. The map wasn't giving him any ideas. He needed ideas and they weren't coming. He tried to force them but that was no good, he knew it was no good and he decided to let them flow in toward him of their own accord.

'The buses,' Gladden said. 'I don't think they'll be watching the buses.'

'When they watch, they watch everything.'

'Don't mind me,' Gladden said. 'I'm new at this.'

'So am I.' He looked at the suitcase at the side of the bench.

'You scared?'

'Sure, I'm scared.'

'We'll get out of it.'

'But meanwhile, I'm scared. I don't want to kid you. I'm really very scared.'

'I know what it is,' Gladden said.

He nodded slowly. 'From last night on the Pike. From today, with Baylock.' He stiffened just a little. 'One thing for certain. We didn't do it. I wanted those cops to live. I wanted Dohmer to live. I wanted Baylock to live. For Christ's sake,' he said, and he saw her gesture, telling him to talk lower, 'I never wanted anyone to die.' He stared ahead, at the people seated in the pavilion, the people on the boardwalk, and indicating them, he said, 'I swear I have nothing against them. Not a thing. Look at them. All of them. I like them. I really like them, even though they hate my guts.' His voice went very low. 'Yours too.'

'They don't know we're alive.'

'They'll know it if we're caught. That's when it starts. When we get grabbed. When we're locked up. That's when they know. It tells them how good they are and how bad we are.'

'We're not bad.'

'The hell we're not bad.'

'Not real bad.' She looked closely at his eyes.

'We're bad enough,' he said. 'Plenty bad.'

'But not as bad as they'll make us out to be. We're not that bad.'

'Try to sell them that.'

'We don't have to sell them anything.' She patted his wrist. 'All we have to do is keep ourselves from getting caught. Because if we don't get caught, they'll never know.'

'But we know.'

'Listen, Nat. We know we didn't do away with anybody. Not today, not last night, not ever. If they say we did, we know they're wrong. That's one thing we know.'

'We can't prove it. But then, suppose we could—?'

'What if we could?' She was looking at him with puzzlement, with something that grew in her eyes and made her eyes wide.

'If we could,' he said, 'it might be worth a try.'

'Nat, don't give me riddles. Tell me what you're talking about.'

'Giving ourselves up.'

'You really thinking about that?'

He nodded.

She said, 'Why are you thinking about it?'

'I don't know.'

'Then stop.'

'I can't,' he said. 'It's there, that's all. I'm

thinking about it.'

'You won't go through with it.'

'I don't know about that, either.'

'Please stop,' she said. 'Please, you're worrying me.'

'I can't help it. I don't want to worry you, but I just can't help it. I'm thinking maybe we ought to do it.'

'No.'

He took her hands and pressed them between his palms. 'Listen to me. I want to tell you something and I want you to listen very carefully.' He pressed tightly on her hands, not knowing how much pressure he was using. With a gesture of his chin he indicated the faces that passed in a thick stream going back and forth along the boardwalk. 'Look at them. Look at the faces. You'd think they have trouble. Trouble? They don't know what real trouble is. Look at them walking. When they take a walk, they take a walk, and that's all. But you and I, when we take a walk it's like crawling through a pitch black tunnel, not knowing what's in front, what's in back. I want to get out of it. I want it to end, there's no attraction and I want it to end.'

She had her eyes closed and she began to shake her head in long, slow swings, her eyes tightly closed. That was all she could do.

‘Listen,’ he said. ‘Like you listen when we talk plans. Listen that way. It’s really the same as a plan, except it’s more clear, it’s open, it’s got more to it than plans. So try to listen to me. We’ll go in. We’ll give ourselves up. We’ll give it to them, put it there in front of them. They’ll go for that. They won’t know what to make of it at first but I’m sure they’ll go for it. We’ll make it plain we could have skipped but instead of skipping and making them come after us we saved them the trouble, we came in. Nobody brought us in. We came in ourselves. We brought ourselves in. That’s like doing the work for them, saving them the headaches, solving it for them, clearing up the business on the Pike, and Baylock in the room. But especially with the Pike. That’s important, the Pike, because it’s always a rough deal when cops die, and other cops always itch to find out who and how and why. So here we’ll be giving it to them and they’ll know, and they’ll understand they’d never know if it wasn’t for us, coming in to tell them how it happened and who did it. And here’s the important thing, the emeralds. We’ll be giving back the emeralds. I know that’ll do some good. Maybe they’ll really go easy on us.’

‘Maybe,’ she said. ‘And maybe. And another maybe.’

'They will,' he insisted. 'I know they'll go easy on us.'

'Easy like a sledgehammer.'

'If we—'

'Now it's if,' she cut in. 'Before it was maybe and now it's if.'

'There's no guarantee. There's never a guarantee. But coming in cold, bringing ourselves in, giving back the emeralds, that sort of thing goes over big. We'll be out in no time.'

Gladden pulled away from him and regarded him quietly, as though looking down on him from a platform. 'You say it, but you don't believe it. You know how long we'll be in.' And then, when he was unable to make a reply, she went on, 'You say we, but you really mean only yourself. I know what you'll do. Because I know you. You'll take the weight of the rap.'

He gave a little shrug. 'I'll get that anyway.'

'No you won't. You'll try to get it. You'll make it as rough on yourself as you possibly can.' She leaned toward him. 'To make it easier for me.' And then slowly, evenly, 'That's only one reason. But there's another.'

He looked at her as though she was something frightening coming toward him, something that was not frightening when he had it covered up deep inside but which was very frightening when it came toward him from the outside.

'You want it,' she said. 'You're aching for it. You'll be glad when they put you in. The longer they keep you in, the better you'll like it.'

He turned his head away from her. 'Quit talking like an idiot.'

'Nat, look at me.'

'Make sense and I'll look at you.'

'You know it's true. You know you want it.'

He tried to say something. The words formed a tight string and the string was broken in his throat.

'You want it,' she said. 'You feel it's coming to you. And you want it.'

Then it was like being in a game of tag and he knew she had tagged and there was no use trying to veer and dodge. He still didn't know what to say. He turned to face her again and saw her wincing and knew it was the look in his eyes that caused her to wince. He tried to pull the look away but it stayed there. All his torture was in the look and it caused her to wince again.

'Please,' she said, 'don't go all to pieces. Try to think clearly.'

There was a moving of gears in his brain. 'I'm thinking very clearly.' And then it came out, the flood of it, the burst of it, the seething. 'I want it because I'm due for it. Overdue. I'm nothing but a no-good God damn thieving son of a bitch and I have it coming to me and I want it.'

'All right.' Her voice was soft, gentle. 'If you want it that much, I want it too. I want whatever you want. We'll get it together.'

He looked at her, waited and wondered what he was waiting for, and gradually realized he was waiting for her to crack. But there was no sign of cracking. All she did was sigh. It was almost like a sigh of relief.

'Now,' he said. 'We won't wait. We'll do it now.' He took her wrists, to help her from the bench, but he saw she wasn't looking at him. She was looking at something else, something behind the bench. He turned his head to see what she was looking at.

He saw the gun. And above the gun, the lips faintly smiling, the aquamarine eyes quietly satisfied, the face of Charley.

CHAPTER XIX

Harbin told himself it was just like sudden bad weather and the bad pattern of it followed the pattern of all the other things that had happened. He knew the aquamarine eyes had watched them as they came out of the hotel, had followed them along the boardwalk, had followed them here, had waited, and Charley had selected the moment. And this was the moment.

The gun showed only enough to let them know it was there, then Charley put it underneath his jacket, the jacket bulging just a little where the muzzle pressed against the fabric. Charley was standing with his back to the rail of the pavilion and now he began to slide himself toward the stairs going down to the beach.

'Come along,' Charley said. 'And don't forget the suitcase.'

Harbin studied the tone of it, caught the trace of hysteria in the tone and knew there was nothing to do but take the suitcase and go along with Charley to the beach. Gladden looked up at him, to see what he wanted her to do. He smiled for her, then he shrugged, and carrying the suitcase he followed her toward the stairs, then down the stairs with Charley's face in front of them as Charley backed his way down to the beach.

The three of them were on the beach. Charley moved around to get the gun pointed at their spines. Charley said, 'Let's take a walk. Let's go look at the ocean.'

They were walking across the beach toward the ocean. The full moon splashed a blue-white glow against the black water. The glow seemed to melt and widen as it came into the beach. It floated onto the beach, a floating of pale blue gauze that took shadow and weaved in and out in front of them as they walked toward the water.

The sand was soft and thick and moved in little hills under their feet. The sound of the ocean, a big sullen sound, blended with the hum and drone coming from the boardwalk. They moved toward the hard wet sand near the water. The boardwalk sound began to fade and as they came onto the damp sand it was all very far away from the boardwalk and away from everything.

'Turn around,' Charley said.

They faced Charley. They saw the shine on the barrel of the gun pointing at them.

Charley made a gesture with the gun. 'Slide the suitcase over here.'

Harbin shoved the suitcase across the sand. Charley picked up the suitcase, felt the weight of it, nodded very slowly and shoved it back toward Harbin.

'Open it,' Charley said.

The gun moved closer to Harbin. He unstrapped the suitcase and opened the lid. He displayed the green flame of the stones and sensed the flame of Charley's eyes looking at the stones. He heard Gladden's breathing. He raised his head and saw the gun and then Charley's face. There was something very unusual in Charley's face. The features seemed completely out of balance.

'Now I got them,' Charley said. 'Now you're giving them to me.'

'All right, take them.'

'Not yet. That wouldn't be proper. Just to make it fair all around I think I'll give you something.'

'You use the gun,' Harbin told him, 'and they'll hear it on the boardwalk. You'll have a thousand people on the beach and you'll be hemmed in.'

Charley moved in closer and the moonlight was full on his twisted features. 'The last time you gave me information, I took it. You pulled my mind away from the suitcase and you had me turning my back on it and walking out of the room. That was a pretty move, and you're a classy engineer. So it means this, it means I can't afford to let you louse me up again.'

'Look, you've got the haul. Why don't you just take it and go away?'

Charley inclined his head so that it rested on his shoulder. His voice was mild. 'You really want me to do that?'

'It's the only thing you can do.'

'And what will you do?'

Harbin shrugged. 'Nothing.'

'You sure?' Charley was smiling. 'You really sure?'

Harbin shrugged again. 'Examine it for yourself. We can't afford to move against you. We're too hot ourselves.'

Charley let out a mild laugh. 'You're real classy, you are. I get a kick from the way you evade an issue. I like the way—' The laugh became sort of wild. 'You know what you want to do.' With the gun he indicated Gladden, his eyes staying on Harbin, his voice jagged. 'You want to get rid of this girl and go back to Della. That's what you want. And I got half a mind to let you do it. I'd like to be with you when you get back there to that room. I want to be there, watching you when you stand there.

When you look at Della. I want to watch your face very close. I want to hear what you have to say. You'll do all the talking because I'll just be standing there, I won't be saying a word. And I know Della won't be talking.'

Harbin felt something slicing into him, felt part of himself being sliced away.

He heard Charley saying, 'Maybe the thing Della liked about you was your class. Maybe that was it. She used to tell me I ought to have more class. She never liked when I talked loud and got excited. You don't talk loud and you don't get excited, so maybe that was what she went for. Whatever it was, she sure went for it. I mean all the way, completely, way up to the point where there I am coming back to the room and I find her sitting on the bed and you're not there. So naturally I want to know what happened, and Della started giving me a story and I know she's giving me a story from the way it's coming out. I see she's in very bad shape and then she started crying and she couldn't talk anymore. So then I knew. I put it together and when I had it together it was too much, and something happened, and I put my hands around her throat. I choked her. I choked Della until she was dead.'

Charley was breathing hard, his face shining above the gun, and suddenly he kicked viciously at the suitcase, sent it over on its side so that the emeralds went flying out and made a green flash and glittered green on the sand.

'I don't want them,' Charley said. He started to weep, loud wrecking weeping. 'I don't care about them, you hear? Only one thing I ever really cared for. I cared for Della. I want her back, you hear?' The weeping was very loud. The heavy tears went running down Charley's face. 'Will I ever find another Della? No. Never. There was only one Della. Now she's dead and I got nothing in my life. But I know this—' Charley lowered his head, his eyes trying to smash Harbin apart. 'I know if it wasn't for you—'

'No, don't,' Harbin pleaded quietly.

'You—'

'Don't.'

'Please don't,' Gladden said. 'Please, Charley, please—'

Charley laughed through the weeping and came moving in with the gun and Harbin saw the split taking place in Charley's brain, saw the brain coming apart as the gun came up in a slanting path that ended when Charley shoved the gun very close. Charley's eyes were opened wide, the white shining like white platters surrounding aquamarine. Then Charley had the gun pressing against Harbin's chest, the finger getting hard on the trigger. Harbin saw it coming, felt it coming, but then it wasn't coming because Gladden moved and brought her arm down on Charley's arm, her weight against Charley, her other arm swinging hard against Charley's face. Harbin was underneath the gun, slamming his shoulder into Charley's groin, getting his shoulder in there solid, pushing and then heaving to knock Charley off his feet and go with Charley to the sand. He was on top of Charley and he reached out and grabbed Charley's wrist and used his own arm as a lever to bend Charley's wrist, bend it back and far back. He saw the gun in Charley's hand, saw the fingers coming loose and away from the gun, saw the gun falling away from the hand, bright blue and in the air, curving and going away and onto the sand. He reached for the gun. Charley hit him in the mouth. He made another try for the gun. Charley hit him again, sent a fist against the side of his hand. He went on reaching for the gun. Charley put two hands around his throat and began to choke him.

He tried to pull his throat away from Charley's hands. He could feel the thumb banging into his jugular vein. The pain was deep, and it went riding up into his eyes. He knew his eyes were starting to bulge. It was difficult to see anything. His mouth fell wide open and his tongue was hanging out. He tried to work his arms but there was no feeling in his arms. All the feeling was in his head now and it was the feeling of going up and back and around and down toward nothing. He could see the sky and the stars, the lights in dark blue, the big dark blue that went sliding slowly, falling toward him but sliding away. And then he heard Gladden.

'Let go,' Gladden said. 'Let go of him.'

He heard the grunt as Charley went on choking him. He felt his head going far to one side and it seemed that his head was being taken away from his body. Then he saw Gladden, and in the same moment he saw the face of Charley hovering over his own face. He saw the gun in Gladden's hand, and all this was very close to his eyes and it blotted out the sky. He heard the shot, saw the flash, felt the choking, heard another shot, saw nothing, felt the choking, and then another shot and then another and Charley's hands came away from his throat. He saw Charley's face and saw Gladden standing there with the smoking gun. That was for just a moment, and after that the sand came up and pounded into his skull.

CHAPTER XX

Gladden had her hands under his arms. She spoke to him but he couldn't make out what she was saying. The pain grew very bad and he didn't think he would be able to get up. Gladden tried to get him up off the sand. His legs were liquid. He had his eyes closed and he was fighting to get up, trying to hear what Gladden was saying.

Then he could hear it as it went in past the pain. She was telling him that he had to get up. Even if he couldn't get up, he had to get up.

'They heard the shots,' she said. 'They're coming.'

He worked with her, came forward to his knees, facing the boardwalk. He saw a rapid movement on the boardwalk, people coming toward the rail and crowding the rail. All along the boardwalk within the range of his vision they were pushing toward the rail, trying to see what had caused the explosive sounds in the darkness of the beach. He had his arm around Gladden's shoulder as she brought him to standing. He looked down and saw Charley.

The moonlight was on Charley and it was rather bright where it came against the head and shoulders. There it seemed to be moving moonlight because the blood was still flowing. Only a small part of Charley's face remained. The rest of it caused Harbin to turn his head fast. He looked at the boardwalk. He saw the moving mob and under the boardwalk lights they were small enamel figures heading toward the various stairways going down to the beach. His head clouded for a moment and he had to close his eyes. When he opened his eyes he saw the gun on the sand near Charley. He turned his head and saw Gladden. She was looking at the boardwalk. Then she looked at the dead man on the sand. Then again at the boardwalk.

'We can't run,' she said. 'There's no use running.'

'We better run. Let's move.'

'Where?' she said. 'Look.' And she pointed up and down along the boardwalk. All along the boardwalk they were coming down the stairways, the stairway directly ahead, the stairways on both sides, then more stairways, and more stairways. Harbin looked at it. He heard the drone of it, the rising sound of droning, and suddenly a sound that split the droning. A sound of whistles. He knew it was police whistles, and something caused him to take another look at the dead man. He told himself the dead man was a policeman and would be eventually identified as a policeman. He knew it meant a very quick decision from any jury, so they had to run, he told himself, but they couldn't run because if they ran they would run into the people and the police coming toward them from the front and from both sides. He looked at Gladden. She had her face turned to the ocean. He took hold of her wrist. His heart began to beat very fast.

'That's it,' he said. 'That's the only way.'

'We'll have to go far out.'

'Very far out.' They were running now, running toward the water, he could see the plan of it, and as the design took shape, he took himself above the pain and the weakness and held himself there as he ran with Gladden toward the water.

'Nat,' she panted. 'Can you swim?'

'You've seen me swim.'

'But now. Can you swim now?'

'Don't worry, I'll swim.' They were on the wet shining sand and she was going ahead of him and then losing stride to wait for him and he said, 'Keep going. Just keep going.'

They ran into the water. They ran through the shallow water where it came in little waves snapping at the beach. The foam of the big waves was thick and very white out there against the black, and they were going toward the big waves, the water up to their knees, the waves breaking just ahead of them. He saw that Gladden still had the hat on, the new hat she had bought in the boardwalk shop. The hat was distinct and bright orange against the black water. He was directly behind Gladden as she threw herself under a wave, and he followed her under the wave, came up alongside her and saw that she still had the hat on.

'Take off the hat,' he said. 'They might see it from the beach.'

'I better take off more than the hat.' She was removing the hat-pin from her hair. 'My shoes feel heavy.'

'Wait until we're further out.' But he knew they couldn't wait very long. His clothes and his shoes were pulling him down. It made him feel as though he were dragging a wagon behind him through the water. He swam ahead of Gladden while she went under the water to take off the orange hat and crumble it and let it sink. He remembered times when Gladden was a kid and he had watched her swim at municipal pools. She had been a smooth little swimmer and swimming was a practice that never went away once it was acquired. It helped some, to know Gladden was a good swimmer. He sent himself under another wave, going under deep, then looked around and saw Gladden swimming toward him. He could see her face clearly against the dark water and she was grinning. He forgot what they were doing out here in the ocean in the night and he figured he was out here with Gladden for some fun and swimming in the Atlantic. Then he felt the drag of his clothes and his shoes pulling him down in the water and he realized what he and Gladden were doing out here, what they were trying to do, and he felt the panic.

He felt the big panic because everything was big. The sky was big and the ocean was big. The waves were very big. The tops of the waves were high above his head, the foam coming like the foaming mouths of big beasts leaping at him. He went under, came up, went under again to slide himself underneath the heavy current of the waves. Gladden came up alongside him and they went under a wave together. Harbin failed to go under deep enough and the rush of the wave caught him full and knocked him off balance. He hit the bottom of the ocean. The panic was there very big and he had a feeling he was several hundred feet down at the bottom of the ocean underneath the night. But coming up he was standing and the water reached only to his chest. He was facing the boardwalk, seeing the lights and the movement of colour against the glow and some vague action on the beach, but that was all. He didn't want to take the time to study it further. He turned and went under another big wave as it came lunging at him. He saw Gladden was some yards ahead and she was swimming nicely. He saw her hair flowing, glowing gold along the black water.

They swam through the waves, went out past the breakers, swimming out and came to the deep water and went on going. They went swimming out, staying close together, concentrating on the swimming. The water was calm out here. Harbin decided it was time to really start swimming and in order to do that they would have to get rid of the clothes and the shoes.

'Hold it,' he said. 'Tread water.'

'You all right?'

'I'm fine. Take off your things.'

They treaded water while they took off their clothes. Harbin had trouble with the shoelaces and he went down a few times and felt the drag of the effort while he struggled with the shoes. Finally he had the shoes off and he liked the free movement of his legs in the water. He took off his clothes and pulled his wallet from the trousers, took the bills from the wallet and pushed them deeply into his socks, so that he could feel the security of the paper money against his ankles and the soles of his feet. He had all his clothes off except his shorts and the socks, with the money in the socks. He thought of the money and it was a good thought, because he knew to what extent they would need the money when they came out of the water.

He wondered when they would come out of the water. He wondered if they would ever come out of the water. That brought the panic again and he began to call himself names for allowing these things to occur to him. He told himself it was going to be all right. That was the only way to look at it, because it was going to be all right. He looked at Gladden. She was grinning. It was the same grin she had given him when they were back there going through the breakers. All at once, staring at the grin, he knew there was something wrong with the grin. It wasn't really a grin. It seemed to be more on the order of a grimace.

'Gladden.'

'Yes?'

'What's wrong?'

'Nothing's wrong.'

'Tell me, Gladden.'

'I tell you nothing's wrong.'

'You tired?'

'Not a bit.' Her face bobbed up and down in the water. She grinned.

'Gladden,' he said. 'Listen, Gladden.' He treaded water toward her. 'We'll work our way out of this.'

'Sure we will.'

'We'll swim out far. We've got to swim out very far.'

'Way out,' she said.

'Very far out. They may look at the water. Maybe they'll look far out.'

'I know.'

'And then,' he said, 'when we're out far enough, we'll turn and follow the line of the beach. We'll do that for a while and then we'll start turning in toward the beach.'

She nodded. 'I get it.'

'We'll come in,' he said, 'where it looks safe.'

'Sure,' she nodded. 'That's the way we'll do it.'

'I've kept the money with me,' he said. 'I've got it right here with me. In my socks. As long as we have the money, we'll manage. There's plenty of money and I know we'll manage.'

'After we come back to the beach.'

'It won't be too long.'

'How long?' She lost the grin, then quickly

picked it up again.

'Not very long,' he said. 'What we've got to do is not get tired. We'll take our time and we won't get tired.'

'I'm not the least bit tired.' The grin became wider. 'I bet it's a very crowded beach right now.'

'Mobbed.' He wanted to look toward the beach but something told him he shouldn't look at it. He knew it would be very far away and he didn't want Gladden to see him looking at the distant beach. He said, 'I guess they're just standing around. Just a mob of them standing around and figuring he probably did away with himself.'

'That's good,' she said. 'That means we're clear.'

'I'm glad you're not tired,' he said. 'Now, look, Gladden—'

'Yes? Yes?'

'If you get tired, I want you to tell me. You hear?'

'All right,' she said. 'I'll tell you.'

'I mean it.' He came in close to her and took a close look at her. 'If you get tired it's important that you tell me right away. We have a lot of swimming to do.'

'All right,' she said. 'Let's start doing it.'

They resumed the swimming. Without the

clothes and the shoes it was easy swimming now and they cut their way through the calm water, going out, the black a thick black ahead of them, nothing ahead of them but the black water and sky, except where the moonlight came against the ocean. The moonlight was far to one side, and it went running slowly along with them as they swam out.

CHAPTER XXI

And as he swam, staying just a little behind Gladden so he could keep his eyes on her and see how she was doing, Harbin began to think about Della. He didn't realize that he was thinking about Della. It was just that Della floated into his mind and began to take control of his mood. More of Della floated in and he saw her somewhere. It was beyond the ordinary.

That was one of the things about Della, her manner of going beyond the ordinary. And yet the basic things she had wanted were really very ordinary. All she had wanted was to be with him in the place on the hill, just be there with him. It couldn't be more ordinary than that.

Certainly she hadn't asked a lot, wanting that.

The golden hair in the water ahead of him came into his eyes and into his mind, pushing softly at Della and sending Della away. He could feel it happening and for a moment he didn't want it to happen. He fought it. But it was happening. Della was going out and away from his mind. He had his thoughts entirely on Gladden.

He called her name. She stopped swimming and he came up close to her. They treaded water.

'What is it?' she grinned at him.

'Want to rest my arms.' But that wasn't it. His arms felt all right. All of him felt all right and he managed to keep himself high above the pain in his throat. He said, 'I want to promise you something. I promise I'll never get ideas like the ideas I had up there on the boardwalk. I mean about giving ourselves up. The way it was, there was a point to it, but now there's no point, no point at all. They'd throw the entire rap at us and we'd have no comeback.

'That's for certain. I took it for granted.' Instead of the grin, she was looking at him in an odd way. 'Why do you tell it to me?'

'Just to let you know.'

She nodded. 'I'm glad you're telling me.'

Then suddenly the grin was there again. 'Really, Nat, you don't have to tell me.'

'Listen,' he said. 'Is anything the matter?'

'Why?'

'What are you grinning about?'

'Grinning?' She worked on the grin and made it fade. 'I'm not grinning.'

'What bothers you?'

'Nothing bothers me,' she said. 'We're out here swimming and after a while we'll go back to the beach.' And again she showed the grin that was not actually a grin.

Then suddenly she was going through the water toward him, her arms were around his neck. 'Hold me,' she said. 'Please hold me.'

He held her. He felt the weight of her and he knew she was forgetting to tread water. He held her up in the water and had the thick wet of her hair against his face.

She said, 'I ruined it. You see what I do? I always ruin it for you. I've always wanted everything to be good for you and I've always made everything bad.'

'That isn't true. I don't want you to say that.'

'Pulling you down. Like I'm pulling you down now. I've always pulled you down.'

'Quit it,' he said. 'Quit it. Quit it.'

'I can't.'

'I want you to quit it. Come away from it.'

'The gun,' she said. 'I can still feel the gun.'

'The gun was a situation. You couldn't help the situation.'

'It feels heavy. I can't let go of it.'

'Now check this,' he told her. 'You had to use the gun. If you hadn't shot the gun, I would have died.'

'That's right.'

'Sure,' he said. 'That's the only way to see it.'

'It was the only thing I could do. I had to use the gun.'

'Of course you had to use the gun.'

'To kill him,' she said.

'To keep him from killing me.'

'But look,' she said, 'I killed him. I killed him.'

'For my sake.'

'No.' And she released herself from Harbin, stepped back through the water, held herself up with a certain lack of effort so it looked as though she was balanced on a platform in the ocean. 'Not for your sake. I wasn't thinking of you. I was thinking of myself. Only of myself. So I shouldn't lose you and that's why I killed him. Not to keep you alive for your own sake, but for my sake. That makes it selfish. Makes it murder. You see what I mean? I murdered him.'

'Don't. Don't please—' and he went to her and held her again.

'No, let go.'

'Gladden—'

'Let go.' She writhed in his arms. Her head went under the water. She pulled her head up from the water and there was a spray. 'Let me go.' It became a shriek. 'Damn you, let go.' She had her hands in his hair, pushing his head back to get him away from her. 'I don't want you to hold me. You hold me as if I'm a child and you're my father.'

Water came into his eyes. He felt dizzy and somehow lost track of what was happening. Then he saw Gladden swimming away. She was swimming very fast. There was a frenzy in the way she swam, going out and away from him. He called to her and told her to stop the crazy swimming. He watched the pace of her swimming and knew she couldn't keep up the pace very long. A little wave hit his face and sent more water into his eyes. Then a lot more water came cutting into his eyes and it was because he had his arms flailing the water, going after Gladden.

But she was going very fast and soon he lost sight of her. He shouted and there was no answer. He shouted again and tried to see her but all there was to see was the black of the water and the sky, and suddenly there was no feeling of direction and he sensed he was getting nowhere. Just then he saw the lights, the thin glowing line of the lamps on the boardwalk. The lights were very far away. He couldn't believe it was that far. The vast distance between himself and the shore lights threw a terrible scare into him and he turned quickly from the sight of the lights. He shouted to Gladden.

There was no answer. He shouted again. His voice went out on a lonely ride across the water and came back to him like a sound in an abyss. He shouted as loud as he could and now he was swimming hard, knowing he had to reach Gladden, knowing deeply and fully true that he had to swim faster because Gladden was far out there and getting exhausted.

His eyes burned into the blackness ahead, trying to see Gladden. All he could see was the blackness. He went on shouting her name as he went on thrashing through the water. The water came into his mouth and choked him. Then, from what seemed like very far away he heard a cry. It was Gladden. She was calling his name. Her voice was faint, and he knew she was in serious trouble. He begged himself to swim faster, hearing Gladden calling to him, knowing Gladden had not been able to think with reason when she swam away from him, knowing her senses had returned in this moment when the trouble came. She was calling to him, asking him to hurry, she needed help. She was drowning.

And then, far ahead of him, there was something golden in the ocean. It was there for a moment and then it wasn't there. He smashed his arms through the water, kicked his way through, saw her golden hair appearing again, saw something white and thin going up on both sides of the golden hair. It was Gladden stretching her thin little arms toward the sky, clutching at the sky, and he knew Gladden was really drowning.

He knew he was swimming much faster than he could really swim. He told himself he would get to Gladden and get to her before she went down, and kept telling it to himself, racing himself toward where he could see the golden hair now flat and smooth on the surface of the ocean, the arms still showing but motionless, and less and less of the arms because the rest of the body was being taken down.

And now all he could see was Gladden's hands above the water. The hands stayed there for just a moment, then went under and there was only the black ahead of his eyes.

Nothingness glided in. He was in the centre

of the nothingness, taken into it, churned by it, going down in it, knowing the feeling of descending. What he saw next was the liquid green, a dark green with circles of light wheeling their way up past his vision. He realized he was swimming down through the water, going down after Gladden. He knew he was going down deep and he told himself to keep going down, get down there to find Gladden. A streak of pain went shooting from his eyes to the back of his head. He wanted to close his eyes. He held his eyes wide open, straining to see Gladden.

He saw her. Off to one side, and floating down easily, very gently going down. Gladden had her head lowered on her chest, her arms away from her body, her gold hair weaving in the green water. He swam down and saw Gladden's arms moving out toward him. It was as though the arms were reaching toward him. He told himself it was too late, he couldn't do anything for her now. They went down very very deep in the water and he realized there was no more air in his lungs. He told himself to hurry and kick his way to the surface. But he saw Gladden's arms reaching toward him, and it was Gladden, it was Gerald's child, and there was only one thing to do, the honourable thing to do. He went down toward

Gladden and got to her and held her and tried hard to lift her and himself up through the water and couldn't do it and they went down together.